"Kevin, you have so much to offer..."

"I wish you'd see that." She smiled. "And just for the record, you're still my hero."

He raised his brows, and a hint of a grin tugged at his mouth. "Lara Donahue, are you flirting with me?"

She managed to contain a smile. "Well, maybe just a little."

He twisted out of her grasp, and within moments, his arm encircled her waist, and he pulled her up next to him. "A girl could get in big trouble flirting like that."

"You're right. She could." Lara stood so close to him that she smelled the mint on his breath and the spicy scent of his cologne.

Kevin narrowed his gaze. "She could even get kissed."

"Well, it's about time!"

His eyes widened with surprise, and Lara laughed.

"I've only been waiting twelve years for you to kiss me." She said it in jest, but her heart had told the truth.

"Why didn't you say something sooner? I'm more than happy to oblige."

ANDREA BOESHAAR was born and raised in Milwaukee, Wisconsin. Married for over 25 years, she and her husband, Daniel, have three adult sons, two of whom are married. Andrea has been writing Christian literature for nearly a decade. For more about Andrea and her work, log onto her Website at: www.andreaboeshaar.com.

HEARTSONG PRESENTS

Don't miss out on any of our super romances. Write to us at the following address for information on our newest releases and club information.

Heartsong Presents Readers' Service
PO Box 719
Uhrichsville, OH 44683

The Long Ride Home

Andrea Boeshaar

Heartsong Presents

To my friends at Froedtert Memorial Lutheran Hospital, especially Kathy M. and Danielle A. and the other wonderful people working in the Emergency and Trauma Center.

A very special thanks to Dusty Rhodes, PRCA clown, and Debra Ullrick for patiently answering my questions and sharing their rodeo expertise with me.

A note from the Author:
I love to hear from my readers! You may correspond with me by writing:

> **Andrea Boeshaar**
> **Author Relations**
> **PO Box 719**
> **Uhrichsville, OH 44683**

ISBN 1-58660-745-6

THE LONG ROAD HOME

All Scripture quotations, unless otherwise indicated, are taken from the HOLY BIBLE, NEW INTERNATIONAL VERSION®.NIV®. Copyright © 1973, 1978, 1984 by International Bible Society. Used by permission of Zondervan Publishing House. All rights reserved.

Our mission is to publish and distribute inspirational products offering exceptional value and biblical encouragement to the masses.

PRINTED IN THE U.S.A.

one

As Lara Donahue penned the date in the departmental log, she shook off the inkling of impending doom. She'd never been a superstitious person. She liked black cats, walked under ladders, and had cracked her share of mirrors. Nothing horrible ever happened to her, and she didn't believe in bad luck. As a Christian, she acknowledged God's will.

So why did she feel so. . .*unsettled?*

As if in reply, her black digital pager squawked out several high-pitched beeps. Lifting it off the scuffed walnut desktop, Lara pressed one of the gadget's four front buttons. A message from Paramedic Base appeared on its tiny screen.

FFL. 29 YR OLD MALE THROWN FROM HORSE.
UNCONSCIOUS. PULSE 85. BP 170/90.
GCS 13. ETA 20 MIN.

Lara grimaced. *FFL*—the Flight-For-Life helicopter—was flying him from the accident site, and the last line of the electronic page indicated their estimated time of arrival to be twenty minutes. The guy must be in bad shape.

Thrown from a horse. . .

Oddly, Lara felt an immediate interest in the new patient. She considered herself a horse lover—had been since junior high school. Now she volunteered at The Regeneration Ranch and taught physically challenged kids how to ride. It was something she looked forward to doing one Saturday out of every month.

5

Lara replaced the pager on her desk and continued logging the patients she'd cared for today. Like poor, old Mr. Drummond. He was an eighty-six year old who obviously had difficulties caring for himself. After a nasty fall down his front porch steps, the older gentleman had been taken by ambulance to County General's emergency department, or "ED." The nurses discovered his personal hygiene was deplorable, his clothes filthy, and his matted white hair infested with head lice. After Mr. Drummond was washed, examined, and diagnosed in good health, aside from his bruised hip, Lara found him a clean shirt and a pair of trousers in the boxes of donations in her office. Next, she implemented his transfer to the neighboring mental health complex where he'd be evaluated further and enrolled in various social programs that might preserve his independence.

Lara ceased her journaling long enough to wish she could take Mr. Drummond home with her. He seemed like such a sweet man. He said his son and two daughters lived too far away to care for him. He was lonely. . .

She shook herself for the second time. What an absurd idea. Of course, she couldn't take home a complete stranger—and she wouldn't. Nevertheless, some cases broke her already bleeding heart.

Lara logged another patient before glancing at her wristwatch. The accident victim would be arriving any minute. As a hospital social worker, she was assigned to the trauma team, which also included a surgeon, residents, nurses, an x-ray tech, chaplain, and registrar, and she was expected to be present when Flight brought in the patient.

Leaving her office, Lara fastened her pager to her skirt's belt, then she headed for the trauma room located on the far side of the emergency department. Walking through the bustling "arena," the center part of the emergency department,

Lara passed the nurses' station. It was an area squared off by gray, faux-marble counters used for writing orders, prescriptions, and documenting in patients' charts. Desktops had been installed inside the parameter and ran along all four of the half-walls. At the helm sat two unit secretaries who answered ever-ringing phones, entered lab and x-ray orders, and paged specialists on call. Outside the emergency room was a four-bed observation unit, with the trauma room positioned cater-corner to it. Just down a short hallway to Lara's left, ambulances pulled into the garage, or ambulance bay, and critical patients could be wheeled through the doors and right into the trauma room. Not-so-critical persons went into ER. When Flight brought in patients, its staff used the nearby service elevators. Everything was set up perfectly, as County General was a "Level One"-trauma facility.

As Lara entered the trauma room, residents and nurses were suiting up in fluid-resistant, disposable gowns, masks, and plastic goggles. The ER doctor and chief neurosurgeon sat in the back, ready to make the necessary calls. Many of the nurses wore lead vests to protect themselves from the harmful rays of the portable x-ray machines. But Lara had no need for a vest. She'd learned to stay out of the way.

Her leather-bound portfolio tucked into the crux of her arm, she found a place to stand and wait for Flight. Within moments, the signal came that the helicopter had landed, and minutes later, the unconscious patient was wheeled in.

Doctors and nurses went to work at once, cutting away clothes and checking vital signs. Lara hadn't gotten a glimpse of the patient, which wasn't at all uncommon. One of the Flight staff handed the registrar the patient's driver's license, and the young woman hurried away to create an account number, wristband, and plastic plate that would be used to stamp up other paperwork and labels for lab work.

Lara opened her portfolio and began to write down specifics on her yellow legal pad.

"This is Kevin," the flight nurse said loud enough for all to hear. A petite woman with short, strawberry blond hair, she wore a blue jumpsuit and spoke in a commanding voice. "He's with a rodeo going on in Waukesha County right now, and he was thrown from a horse."

Lara frowned as the name struck a familiar chord in her memory. She'd known a guy named Kevin who competed in the rodeo circuit. They'd grown up in the same neighborhood, and he'd been the one who sparked her love for horses when she was thirteen years old.

That awkward time in her life flashed across her mind, and Lara recalled her pudgy frame traipsing after tall, blond, and extremely cute Kevin Wincouser, who patiently taught Lara everything he knew about riding and grooming horses. He hadn't been required to spend time with her—he was four years older, on the football team, and popular with all the girls in school. But since their parents were well acquainted, attended the same church, and lived in the same neighborhood, Kev was kind enough to show Lara "the ropes," so to speak.

Eighteen months later, a year after his parents were tragically killed overseas, Kev took off for the excitement of the rodeo, and his younger brother moved in with an aunt and uncle in a neighboring state. That was over a decade ago, and nobody had seen the Wincouser boys since.

This couldn't be the same guy. . .

Danielle, the registrar, returned and handed Lara the driver's license along with a sticker on which the patient's account number, medical record number, and date of birth had been printed.

"There are some folks in the lobby asking about this patient," she told Lara. The attractive African-American woman handed off the rest of her paperwork to the ER technician. Pausing near Lara again, she added, "I told 'em you'd be out in a few minutes."

"Thanks."

Holding up the driver's license, Lara looked at the patient's name. Her heart sank. It *was* him! Kevin Wincouser!

Oh, Lord, I can't believe it. . .

She glanced across the room where medical personnel still assessed Kevin's injuries. She felt numb and in shock. Nevertheless, Lara knew she had to be a professional despite the sudden personal angle in this situation. She forced herself to concentrate on the team's ongoing evaluation and take notes. Minutes later, Kevin was wheeled off for a CT scan, and the trauma room emptied out.

Collecting herself, Lara made her way over to the neurosurgeon. "What's your initial diagnosis, Dr. LaPont? The patient has friends and/or family members in the lobby, and I'll have to tell them *something*."

"Well, we're obviously looking at a head injury," the physician said. He towered over Lara by nearly a foot, and the way he combed his straight dark brown hair forward gave the specialist a somewhat ominous appearance. "I won't know for sure until I get the CT results."

"All right, I'll relay that message."

Closing her portfolio, Lara headed for the lobby. She feared the worst for Kevin. He might have suffered a brain injury. Would he ever be the same? Many times, head injury patients never fully recovered, although Lara couldn't help but be hopeful. Medical advancements had come a long way.

And, of course, the Lord was able to do exceeding, abundantly, and above, in the way of healing. The Kevin Wincouser Lara once knew had been a committed Christian, although his dedication to the Lord seemed to have waned after his parents' deaths. Had Kevin ever renewed his faith?

Making her way back through the arena, Lara's mind whirred with questions. She wondered if Kevin had married. Was his wife among the people waiting for an update on his condition? She steeled herself, planning what to say and what not to say.

Lara reached the emergency department's waiting area and walked down the center aisle until she came to a small cluster of people. To her right, she spotted a clown dressed in dusty denims and a red, white, and blue striped shirt. His face had been painted with colorful makeup, and on his head, he wore an over-sized Stetson. He was juggling for some kids who cackled at his antics. The lobby suddenly looked like the circus had come to town.

Make that the rodeo.

"Any of you here for Kevin?" Lara asked, careful not to use his last name and violate patient confidentiality laws.

The clown ceased his act, and two cowboys stood along with a woman. Turning to face Lara, she stepped forward. Petite and slender, wearing blue jeans that were as snug as a second skin, she tossed her head, sending a thick lock of auburn hair over her shoulder.

"Mackenzie Sabino." She extended her right hand. "I'm with Kevin. Are you the doctor?"

"No." Lara took her hand in a quick, polite introductory greeting. "I'm a social worker. I just wanted to give you a brief update. The doctor will be out shortly, and he can give you more details." Lara pointed to a door at the end of the waiting room where they could speak in private. "Please follow me."

Lara drew a set of keys from her skirt pocket and unlocked the door to the "quiet room." It was a place where friends and relatives of trauma victims could sit and talk—sometimes cry—and not be gawked at by the general public.

"Please make yourselves comfortable. Can I get you anything? Coffee? Soda?"

The redheaded female whirled around. "Look, Miss *Whoever-you-are*, I don't want anything except news about Kevin, got it?"

"Whoa, Mac, take it easy," one of the cowboys said, grabbing hold of her elbow and reining her in. "This little lady's just tryin' to be nice."

The woman raised a doubtful brow.

Lara felt herself tense. "I apologize. I didn't introduce myself. My name is Lara Donahue." She met the other woman's intense gaze but kept her voice low and even. Wife, fiancée, or maybe just a friend, Mackenzie Sabino was probably sick with fear over Kevin's well-being. Everyone handled stress in a different way. Lara had learned that much in the last two years on the job. "Mr. Wincouser is having a CT scan right now. Once the results come back, the neurosurgeon will discuss them with you." Lara tipped her head. "Are you his wife?"

"Possibly."

The clown laughed, a deep, jolly sound. "In your dreams, Mac." He chuckled once more, and the two cowboys joined him.

"Shut up, you guys." Mac whirled on her heel and walked several feet away from them.

"She's Wink's rodeo sponsor," the clown informed Lara.

"Wink?" Lara frowned in confusion.

The cowboy grinned. "Yeah, that's what we call him."

"Oh. . .I see."

Lara chastened herself for feeling relieved to learn the woman wearing the tight jeans and snobbish demeanor wasn't Kevin's wife. Kevin's taste in women wasn't any of Lara's business. Sponsor or wife. . .why should she care? She hadn't even seen him in over a decade.

Except she'd practically grown up with the Wincouser boys. Lara couldn't help feeling worried about Kevin.

Forcing herself back into her professional mode, she lowered herself onto the plaid sofa. She opened her portfolio and took out a pen. "Would you mind telling me what happened today? How did the injury occur?"

Mackenzie gave her an indignant look. "He got bucked off a horse. What more is there to tell?" She raised her arms in exasperation.

"Aw, Mac, take it easy, will ya?" the second cowboy said, taking a seat in a tan leather armchair adjacent to Lara. He appeared to be younger than the other two men. His blondish brown hair was shaved in the classic crew-cut style. "Wink is a two-time world champion bareback rider, and he was riding as good as ever today. Stayed on the bronc for the entire eight-second ride. But the horse must have calmed down some, and Wink relaxed enough so when the horse started bucking again, Wink flew off like a rag doll."

Lara grimaced, imagining the scenario.

"He didn't stay on for eight seconds," Mackenzie Sabino spat with sarcasm. "He fell off just before the buzzer." She cursed. "And now with this injury, he's going to be out points and money."

Lara's mouth fell open, knowing Kevin stood to lose so much more.

"Don't mind her," the other cowboy said with a little smile. He sat down and held his black, wide-brimmed hat between his knees. His face was tanned, and his hair was the color of cherry wood. "Mac's mouth tends to run faster than her mind."

"Oh, quiet," she snapped. "I don't need you making excuses for me."

"Someone's gotta do it," the younger cowboy mumbled under his breath.

"I heard that, Jimmy."

The clown took the chair beside the quipping cowboy and grinned at Lara. "So how is Wink *really* doing? C'mon now. You can tell us."

"I honestly don't know. The doctor is waiting for the CT scan results."

"Do you have a business card, Honey?" the older of the two cowboys asked.

Taken aback by the way she'd been addressed, Lara glanced at the man across from her, noting for the first time his very rugged appearance. From the tips of his well-worn boots to his daring, brown-eyed gaze, he seemed every inch the classic cowboy. She suspected he called every woman, "Honey."

Lara pulled a card from her portfolio and wondered if the guy didn't believe she was whom she claimed. After handing it to him, he seemed to study it for several long seconds before dropping it into the breast pocket of his white pin-striped shirt.

"This is a very nice hospital," the clown remarked.

Lara sensed he was attempting polite conversation, so she did the same. "We take very good care of our patients here."

"That's good to know."

The other cowboy with the cropped hair cleared his throat. "You mentioned a neurosurgeon. . .that doesn't sound too good."

"The neurosurgeon is part of the trauma team that responds to head injuries."

"See, Jimmy, just a formality," the clown said.

Mackenzie Sabino had taken to pacing the carpeted floor behind Jimmy and the clown. "I can't believe it. I'm going to have to cancel the television interview for tomorrow," she muttered, "and after I worked so hard to get Wink on that local morning show too."

Lara's pager chirped, and she snatched it off her belt and

read the phone number on the screen. *8745*. She recognized it as the trauma room's extension.

"Excuse me while I make this call." She stood and smiled at the clown and cowboys before crossing the room and plucking the receiver from the wall phone. She dialed the number, and after two rings, one of the nurses answered her call.

"Dr. LaPont is taking the head injury patient to surgery. He started to go downhill in CT, and it looks like he's got a head bleed."

Lara closed her eyes as regret filled her soul. "All right. I'll let his friends know it might be a long night."

"Good. And let them know that after surgery, he'll go to the NICU."

"Okay. Thanks."

Lara hung up the phone. Pivoting, she at once became aware of the curious faces staring back at her.

"I'm sorry to tell you this, but. . .Kevin. . .he's on his way to surgery right now. He's got what we call a subarachnoid hemorrhage or, in simpler terms, some bleeding in his brain. The neurosurgeon will go in and—"

"Brain surgery?!" Mackenzie shrieked. "He'll be nothing but a. . .a vegetable! He'll never ride again!"

"Oh, now, calm down, Mac," the clown said. "It's not like they're doing a lobotomy. Surgeons can perform amazing things nowadays. Wink'll be back to his old self in no time." He turned and gave Lara a wide, white-painted smile. "Isn't that right?"

She smiled back and nodded, praying it was true.

two

In a dream-like state, Kevin floated through space and time. Peace flooded his being like the perfect drug. He felt full and satisfied as though he'd just gobbled down a bountiful Thanksgiving Day meal. He felt weightless, confident, and competitive, and imagined he was about to take the ride of his life.

"He that has an ear, let him hear what the Spirit says. . ."

What?

Kevin tried to discover where the voice had come from, but his limbs felt restricted somehow. That tranquil feeling vanished, and he suddenly felt trapped.

"Those whom I love I rebuke and discipline. So be earnest and repent."

A wave of panic engulfed Kevin. He recognized the scriptural passage, but it had been years since he'd cracked open a Bible. He'd decided long ago that religion didn't work. Look where it got his devout parents. Dead. Instead, Kevin chose to be the decider of his own fate. He lived life hard and fast, and he knew he was no saint. Experience had taught him that sinners had a lot more fun.

But was God really talking to him now?

Naw. Couldn't be. This was just some weird dream.

On the other hand, if it wasn't, Kevin figured he was in for a heap of trouble. What could God want with him except to pour out His wrath and judgment?

"For I know the plans I have for you…plans to prosper you and not to harm you, plans to give you hope and a future."

Kevin knew that verse. He memorized it as a teenager. But that was a lifetime ago. He wasn't the same person anymore.

"You did not choose me, but I chose you and appointed you to go and bear fruit—fruit that will last."

Not me, God. You've got the wrong guy for that job.

The reply couldn't even take root for, all at once, Kevin felt himself free-falling downward, like a man who'd just jumped from an airplane without a parachute. Fear gripped every muscle and robbed him of his next breath.

Help me! Help me! Don't let me fall like this! God, please help me!

૪

Lara glanced at her watch. Seven o'clock. This wasn't exactly the way she had planned to spend her Friday night. However, she couldn't get herself to leave the hospital without knowing Kevin was all right. Earlier, she had shown his friends to the Family Center where they could wait out the long and delicate procedure in some comfort. With that accomplished, Lara had returned to the ED where she finished her work. After a couple of hours of overtime, she made her way up to the Neurological Intensive Care Unit, or NICU, where she planted herself next to Polly Nivens, a unit secretary and one of Lara's good friends.

"I'm off work in a half-hour," Polly said, "and I have no intentions of hanging around."

Lara shot her brunette friend a look of irritation. "I'd wait with you if you were in my situation."

"Yeah, I suppose you would." Reluctance laced her tone.

Lara grinned. She and Polly had been hired around the same time and met during their orientation week here at County General. They'd hit it off and, with so much in common, such as their Christian faith, they'd remained friends ever since. Together, they had even joined a local Christian singles' group that met once a month. Some of the situations that occurred during those get-togethers kept Lara and Polly laughing until the next month's meeting.

"Well, maybe we won't have to hang around too long after your shift. I called the recovery room," Lara said, "and one of the nurses told me Kevin would be out of the OR soon. That was an hour ago. I imagine he'll be brought up here to the unit any time now."

Polly shrugged in reply as she separated paperwork.

Lars smiled and watched her friend complete her task. Wearing light blue scrubs with a colorful cotton cover-up, Polly stood an average five-feet four and had average proportions. She and Lara shared a similar figure—although they both admitted they'd like to shed a good twenty pounds. They swapped articles of clothing, an inexpensive way to enhance each other's wardrobe, and they tried all types of diets. However, the latter more often than not resulted in a drive to Snoopy's ice cream parlor after a stressful day where they ordered double scoops of "Death-by-Chocolate."

In fact, if Snoopy's were open right now, Lara would be tempted to order a triple chocolate sundae or a banana split.

"Are you thinking of your friend?" Polly asked with a sympathetic note in her voice.

Lara laughed. "No, I'm thinking about how much I need an ice cream fix."

"Oh, yeah, that'd be good. I wonder what the Friday Flavor was today." Opening her desk drawer, Polly removed a menu from Snoopy's. "Cherry Cheesecake. Good, we didn't miss much."

"We're hopeless," Lara stated, shaking her head and smiling. "I know it."

Untwisting the cap on her diet cola, Lara took a drink. The sugar-free beverage would have to suffice for now. Looking over at Polly again, she decided to change the subject. "What do you think the odds are that Kevin Wincouser would be flown to this hospital and I would be the social worker on call and in the trauma room?"

"Not very likely, but when God's involved, there are no such things as coincidences."

"I agree, but I'm too much in shock to think about what God might have in store for the future. I've been praying so hard that Kevin will be okay."

"What do you think you'll say to him when he wakes up? 'Where have you been all my life?'?"

"Oh, quiet." Lara cast an exasperated glance toward the ceiling. She and Polly had been admiring Kevin's picture on his Missouri State driver's license. Judging by his photo, Kevin had gone from a cute boy to a rakishly handsome man. And how many men—women too—ever looked so good on their driver's licenses? Those government snapshots always seemed to capture people at the worst possible angles.

But not Kevin's.

"You know, seriously, Polly, I hope I get the chance to thank him for sharing his knowledge about horses with me. It's because of him that I've been able to teach my kids how to ride."

"Your kids?" Polly grinned. "That's neat how you refer to them. You're a true saint for volunteering your time over at the ranch. Handicapped kids require a lot of patience."

"You're more than welcome to join me any time."

Polly chuckled. "Yeah, so you've told me. . .about a hundred times. Maybe even two hundred. The problem is, I'm lacking in the patience department."

"Maybe God will teach you patience when you donate your time."

Polly gave her a skeptical look.

At that moment, a transporter and a nurse from recovery

wheeled a gurney through the doors of the NICU.

"Is that Room Seven?" Polly asked.

"Sure is," the husky transporter replied.

Lara strained to get a look at Kevin, but all she could see was his bandaged head. Minutes later, Bill Kitrell, one of Dr. LaPont's residents, walked in. He slapped down the metal-encased chart. Without a word, he began to write out orders.

"Hey, Bill, is the guy in seven going to be all right?" Polly asked, stealing the words right off the tip of Lara's tongue.

"Yeah, I think so," the young man said without even glancing up.

"I'm asking because Lara grew up with him."

Bill raised his dark head and peered at Lara. "Oh, yeah?"

She nodded.

The soon-to-be neurosurgeon, a nice—and very married—guy, gazed at the chart again. "I was wondering what you were still doing here. Although. . ." He cast a hooded glance in Polly's direction. "I know you two are cohorts, so I didn't think too much about it."

"Cohorts?" Polly put her hands on her hips. "Who uses that word in this day and age?"

"I just did. Didn't you hear me?" He slid the chart in Polly's direction.

"A wee bit crabby tonight, eh, Bill?"

"Just a little," he confessed. "I haven't slept in two days."

"Is it all right if I go in and see Kevin?" Lara asked, interrupting the banter.

"Sure." Bill forced a tight smile. "But your friend is in a coma-induced state, and we're keeping him that way for a while to make sure no more swelling occurs in his brain."

Lara stood and stepped out of the nurses' station, only to glimpse several RNs at work in Kevin's room. She paused, deciding to wait until they had him settled.

"Bill, has anyone been to the Family Center to let Kevin's friends know he's out of surgery?"

"Yeah, I think LaPont went down there." He gave both ladies a curt nod. "Now if you'll both excuse me, I need to catch a few winks."

The word "wink" reminded Lara of Kevin's nickname. She straightened and glanced into his room again. The nurses were just finishing up. She walked to the doorway, and the male RN waved her in.

"Working overtime, aren't you? I don't think this fellow's up for an interview."

Lara smiled at the glib remark. Since her assigned areas as a social worker consisted of the emergency department and the three intensive care units, she was recognized by most of the personnel who worked there. "This is actually a personal call."

The nurse, lanky blond with a goatee, suddenly looked concerned. "Is this patient a friend of yours?"

"Yes. A friend from the past. I haven't seen him in about ten years."

"Tough way to get reacquainted," the other RN said as she peeled off her protective gloves. Without waiting for a reply, the slender woman with short, light-brown hair and pock-marked complexion brushed past Lara.

Stepping over to Kevin's bedside, Lara cringed at all the ticking, pulsing machinery and plastic tubing coming and going from various parts of his body. He'd been placed on a ventilator to help him breathe, and the IV fluid that kept him hydrated and nourished ran into his arm. Surgical staff had bandaged his head so Kevin appeared to be wearing a white cap. His face resembled the Kevin Wincouser Lara used to know, and contrary to the celebrity smile on his driver's license, his expression was now one of unconscious bliss.

The other nurse left, and Lara touched the back of Kevin's

hand. Compassion engulfed her. *Oh, Lord, please heal this man. I have no idea what sort of person he is now, but he was nice to me at a time when a lot of other kids weren't.*

Lara could still recall how some of the boys in the neighborhood called her "Larda," poking fun at her chubby size. But neither Kevin nor his brother ever taunted and teased her. The Wincouser boys had always been kindhearted and polite.

She stood there a few more moments before giving herself a mental shake. She felt suddenly exhausted and knew it was time to go home. At least she'd learned Kevin had made it through surgery, and according to Bill Kitrell, he would recover.

Leaving his room, Lara made her way over to where Polly stood gathering her belongings. The third-shift unit secretary had arrived and appeared busy at the computer.

"Ready to leave?" Polly asked. "I sure am!"

Lara nodded, and together, she and Polly walked out of the NICU. They reached the elevator, and Lara suddenly remembered she had Kevin's driver's license.

"Pol, I need to stop at the Family Center. I should return Kevin's license to his friends."

"Okay. I'll go with you so neither of us has to brave the parking structure alone."

"Great."

Rounding the corner, the two women ambled into the surprisingly busy Family Center. Lara glanced around and spotted Dr. LaPont on the telephone nearby, but she didn't see anyone of the four people who had been in the emergency department earlier. Once LaPont finished his call, Lara managed to catch his attention as he started to head out the door.

"No one's here with the patient," the surgeon informed her. "I even had them paged overhead. I don't have a phone number. Nothing."

"That's odd. I got the impression Kevin's friends were going to stick around until he came out of surgery."

LaPont shrugged, then proceeded to give Lara the rundown on Kevin, all of which she'd heard from the resident.

"If I see his friends, I'll be sure to tell them," she said, wondering how she'd manage to keep her promise since she was off for the weekend.

Dr. LaPont inclined his head in a parting nod, then left the Family Center.

Feeling helpless, Lara looked at Polly who shrugged.

"Nice friends."

Lara groaned. "If Kevin is from Missouri, like his driver's license states, then he's a long way from home. I don't have a clue as to whether he has family. . .a wife. He could be married with five kids for all I know."

"That'd be a bummer." Polly's green eyes shimmered with the jest.

Lara couldn't help but laugh as they headed for the employee parking structure on the other side of the hospital. "I must confess, I did have a crush on Kevin my freshman year of high school. He was a senior, and every time he saw me in the hallway, he'd wave or smile or say hello." Lara chuckled at the recollection. "I was the envy of all the freshman girls—maybe even *all* the girls."

"He sounds like he was a nice guy back then. I wonder if he's still a nice guy."

"Don't know." Lara hitched her purse strap up higher onto her shoulder. "Doesn't seem like he has very nice friends."

"Maybe they went to get something to eat. If they come back, they can call Admitting and find out where Kevin is, although they won't be allowed in the NICU at this time of night. Maybe someone told them that, so they left."

"Yeah, maybe. . ." Lara thought it over. "Do you think

they'll know to call the admitting department?"

"Well, if they don't, it's not your problem, Lara. You're off duty now—you have been for the last six and a half hours."

"I know, but—"

"But you knew the guy way-back-when. . .I understand, except it's still not your problem. Who's the social worker on call this weekend?"

"Sarah Jackson."

"Good. It's Sarah's problem, and since it's our weekend off, we're going to enjoy it!"

Stepping out into the balmy June night, Lara pushed out a smile. She agreed with everything Polly told her; however, her heart didn't seem to be listening. Kevin Wincouser was her "problem." The niggling deep inside her chest told her so. What's more, she had an odd feeling that he would likely be her problem until some family member claimed him.

three

"What's the matter, Muffin? You seem a million miles away this morning."

Lara snapped out of her musings and realized she'd been staring sightlessly into her coffee cup. Lifting her gaze, she smiled at her grandmother who was spreading jam across her slice of toast. "Guess I've been a rude breakfast companion."

"Not at all. You obviously have a lot on your mind."

"Yeah, I do." Lara looked back down into her black coffee.

"Anything you'd like to talk about?"

Lara considered the offer. She'd been thinking about Kevin ever since Flight-for-Life flew him into the ED yesterday, and now, this morning, she wondered how to get in touch with his friends. She supposed she could drive out to the rodeo in Waukesha. It wasn't all that far away. What gnawed at her was the fact she hadn't gotten the chance to say she and Kevin knew each other as kids and. . . Were they going to contact Kevin's brother, Clayt? Somebody should!

"Gram, do you remember the Wincousers?" Lara warned herself to be careful. If she said too much, she'd violate patient confidentiality laws. Looking up from her coffee, she peered into her grandmother's face with its delicate features bordered by white hair that she wore in a short, classy style.

"The Wincousers. . .yes, of course I remember them. Ted and Roberta were the ones killed in that tragic train wreck in Japan, isn't that right?"

Lara nodded.

"And they had two sons, both fine young men, if I recall."

Gram took a sip of her freshly brewed green tea. "I wonder what ever happened to them."

"Kevin left to compete in the rodeo." That hadn't been a secret. Lara recalled hearing her parents discussing the topic in hushed voices. The pastor had been unsuccessful in talking Kevin out of moving away. Various other well-intentioned church people tried to dissuade him also, but Kevin seemed determined to leave Wisconsin.

"He was the older boy, right?"

"Right."

"Seems to me he took his parents' deaths extraordinarily hard."

"That's what I heard too."

Gram bit into her toast, chewed, and swallowed. Then one of her light brows dipped in a frown. "Why are you thinking about the Wincousers?"

"Oh, something happened yesterday that caused me to remember them. I can't go into details, though."

"I see."

Lara scooted her chair back and stood. Lifting her cereal bowl and coffee mug off the kitchen table, she carried them to the sink.

"Don't worry about the dishes, Muffin, I'll take care of them."

"Thanks, Gram. I've got some errands to do, and the sooner I leave the better."

"Well, then, don't let breakfast dishes keep you."

Smiling, Lara kissed her grandmother's cheek before ambling down the hallway of the spacious flat they shared. The lower half of the duplex was occupied by Lara's parents and her younger brother, Tim. An older sister lived on the other side of town with her husband and their three small children.

Entering the large bathroom with its white ceramic-tiled

floor, Lara shed her nightgown and stepped into the tub and turned on the faucet. She heard the familiar knocking of the pipes before she pulled up the knob activating the overhead shower.

Lara had grown up in this house. It had been built in the 1930s, and even with remodeling and updates, some things never changed, like noisy plumbing and handcrafted charm. When she was a kid, Lara's grandparents and Aunt Eileen lived up here, but since then, Gramps had gone to be with the Lord, and Eileen had moved to Colorado where she remained happily unmarried and now taught high school science. Over the past few years, Gram's health declined, so Lara volunteered to move in with her. The elderly woman enjoyed the company, and Lara liked caring for her, the little bit that she did. Gram was still quite self-sufficient for the most part.

After washing up, Lara padded to her bedroom. Gram had insisted she take the master bedroom when she moved in, and seeing it would do no good to argue, Lara agreed. She painted and wallpapered to make the room feel like her own. In fact, the entire flat was beginning to look like "her own," but Gram adored the changes.

Once she'd dressed in jeans and a blue-and-red striped T-shirt, Lara gathered her light brown hair, with its blond highlights, and clipped it up at the back of her head. Snatching her purse off the desk in the living room, she called a goodbye to Gram and left. As she passed the downstairs unit, Lara opened the backdoor and hollered a greeting.

"Anybody need anything while I'm out?"

"Don't think so," her father answered from the direction of the living room.

Lara continued on her way out. Behind the off-white vinyl-sided house with its burgundy shutters and next to the garage, her father had erected a carport under which Lara and Tim parked their vehicles. Unlocking the door of her teal compact car, Lara climbed in and started the engine. Next, she backed into the alley, deciding her first stop would be the hospital. Lara hoped she'd find Kevin's friends there so she wouldn't have to search for them at a crowded rodeo.

When she arrived at County General, Lara was unprepared for the sight that met her in the spacious lobby. Television crews and cameras filled the area, and several feet away, Lara recognized the Director of Public Relations talking to media personnel.

She took cautious steps forward, wondering what was going on. Then someone caught her elbow, and Lara whirled around to face a man about fifty years of age with a stocky build, graying brown hair, and a suntanned face.

"You don't recognize me without my makeup, do you?" He laughed. "I'm Quincy Owens, otherwise known as 'Quincy the Clown.'?"

Lara blinked until finally the realization struck. "Oh. . .from yesterday. Kevin's friend."

"That's right." Quincy smiled then nodded toward the reporters. "This here's the press conference Mac arranged right after Wink went into surgery. She's determined to make him famous one way or another."

"Oh. . .so that's what's going on here."

"Yep. We're all gettin' updated on Wink's condition. The doctors say he's going to be okay, even though he's in a coma right now."

Lara noticed the worry lines that formed on Quincy's forehead.

"I sure hope he's okay. . ."

"I hope so too." Lara opened her purse and pulled out her wallet. From it, she extracted Kevin's driver's license. "I need to return this." She handed the plastic card to Quincy. "The registrar in the emergency department gave it to me yesterday, and somehow I never gave it back. I apologize."

After giving the ID a quick glance, Quincy handed it right back. "Maybe you oughta keep it till Wink wakes up. See, the rodeo is over after tomorrow. We're all pulling up stakes and heading out. Wink'll have to catch up with us when he's better."

"What about his sponsor. . .Mac?"

The large man shrugged. "She might stick around. Her daddy's company has a lot of dough riding on Wink. . .pardon the pun."

"I see. . ."

"You can give the license to Mac, if you want, although she's not the most responsible person in the world."

Lara slipped the driver's license back into her purse. "I'll find out where Wink. . .I mean, Kevin's belongings are. Security will know. I'll be sure to add his license to his other things."

"Sounds good."

After a hesitant look, she decided to forge on. "I never got a chance to tell you and the others that Kevin and I grew up in the same neighborhood right here in Milwaukee—Wauwatosa, actually. Our part of town borders Waukesha County."

Quincy brought his chin back. "I never knew Kevin was from around here." He turned. "Did you know that, Brent?"

"What?"

Several feet away, another man pivoted and looked their way. Lara recognized him as the ruggedly handsome cowboy who had asked for her business card.

"Woman here says she grew up with Wink. I didn't know he hailed from Wisconsin, did you?"

The man called Brent sauntered over. He gave Lara an appraising glance from head to toe before meeting her gaze. A blush warmed her face.

"Yeah, I knew Wink was from Wisconsin. Didn't realize it

was this particular area, though." He tore his stare from hers and looked at Quincy. "But if she says he is, I imagine it's true."

Lara felt oddly flattered that Brent would give her the benefit of the doubt.

"I can't imagine there's more than one Kevin Wincouser in the world," Lara added, "at least not one who's twenty-nine years old and in the rodeo."

"Heaven help us if there is," Brent quipped with a slight grin.

Quincy chuckled.

Pulling something from the breast pocket of his plaid shirt, he offered it to Lara. An instant later, she realized he'd handed her two tickets.

"Bull-riding competition is tonight. Want to come watch?"

"Um. . ."

"Bring a friend."

Lara glanced at the thick blue tickets before looking back at Brent. She couldn't think of any other commitments she had this evening.

"You do have a friend, don't you?"

"Huh? Oh, yeah. . ." She shot him an exasperated frown. "Of course I have a friend."

Brent shifted his weight. "Just one? Or do you need more tickets?"

Lara smirked. She was beginning to understand the man's sarcastic wit. "My brother and his fiancée might like to come."

Brent pulled out two more tickets from his shirt pocket.

"My sister, her husband, and their three kids—"

"I said 'friends,' not your entire relation."

Lara laughed. "I'm just giving you a hard time. Four tickets are plenty. Thanks."

Quincy stood by chuckling. "And notice she didn't even mention a husband, Brent."

"I noticed."

A twinkle entered his brown eyes, and Lara could feel another blush burn into her cheekbones. She had a feeling Brent probably charmed the ladies from coast to coast. But he certainly seemed nice enough.

"Well, thanks for the tickets."

"Don't let 'em go to waste, now," Quincy the Clown said with a grin.

"I won't. I promise."

With a smile, Lara walked past the men and into the throng of media people. The press conference had just finished, and Lara realized, much to her disappointment, she would now have to wait until the evening news to hear what was said publicly about Kevin Wincouser's medical condition.

four

"Do I look okay to go to the rodeo?"

Standing in her bedroom, Lara scrutinized Polly's outfit, faded jeans and a red sweater. "You look fine. It's not like the rodeo is a black-tie affair or something."

"I know, but. . ." She pushed out a pretty pout. "I don't even own a pair of boots. I'm wearing athletic shoes. Some cowgirl I am."

Lara laughed. "Don't worry about it. There'll be plenty of folks in athletic shoes tonight. You'll see."

"Well, you look like a cowgirl."

Lara turned to gaze at herself in the full-length mirror attached to the closet door. She'd chosen a blue plaid, light-weight, long-sleeved shirt and a newer pair of denim jeans. But unlike Polly, Lara had boots.

"I'm feeling out of sorts here," her friend confessed.

"Want to change?"

"I thought you'd never ask. Yes!"

Grinning, Lara swung open her closet door and helped Polly select a soft chambray shirt. Lara found an old pair of brown boots that had obviously seen better days, but Polly accepted the offer to wear them despite the leather's many scuffs and scrapes.

"Now, I feel like I'm dressed for the rodeo," Polly declared, admiring her outfit in the mirror. "Yee-ha! Let's go."

Laughing, the girls walked down the hallway, heading for the back door. Lara called a farewell to her grandmother who sat in the living room watching reruns of *The Lawrence Welk Show*.

Outside, the setting sun cast golden hues against the cloudless evening sky. Lara decided to drive, so they walked to her car and climbed in.

"So this Brent is really a hunk, eh?" Polly asked, snapping her seatbelt into place.

"I don't believe I ever used the word *hunk*." Lara grinned and backed out of the carport, then drove down the alley. "But he is quite the charmer."

"Aren't all cowboys charming? I mean, when I think cowboys I think of that cute actor in that recent Western. . . . What's his name?"

"I can't remember his name, but I know which one you're talking about, and Brent strikes me the same way. Hollywood handsome. But he's almost too charming for his own good."

"Well, you know, looks can be deceiving. Maybe the guy is really an upstanding Christian who adheres to good moral values."

"Yeah, maybe."

Lara wanted to be careful. She wasn't a prude, and she knew she ought not to pass judgment; however, God wanted her to be discerning. There was nothing wrong with handsome and charming—unless it went along with boozing and womanizing. Lara had heard too many tales involving the latter, especially when it came to rodeo cowboys, and it caused her to be suspicious of Brent's motives.

"Tim once told me that some guys see an innocent woman as a challenge."

"Oh, what does your brother know? He's a committed Christian with a sweet fiancée. Besides, how would Brent know you're *innocent*?"

"I think men can tell, Polly."

She merely shrugged.

Lara decided there was no point in debating the issue. She

wanted to have fun tonight. "Personally, I think the reason Brent turned on his charm and gave me free tickets to the rodeo is because he wants me to spend money there—and bring some friends who'll spend money too."

"Bingo. I think you're right."

Lara laughed. The good times were already beginning.

A half-hour later, they arrived at the fairgrounds, paid to park, then walked through the dusty gravel parking lot to the arena with a crowd of other people. After a quick stop in the restroom to brush their hair and touch up their lipstick, Lara and Polly were headed out to find their seats. An usher came forward and offered his assistance, handing them both a program. Lara and Polly were soon shocked to discover that their "tickets" were actually VIP passes and that they would watch the bull-riding competition from the stands right behind the bucking chutes.

"We're going to be able to hear the bulls snort from these seats," Lara teased.

"Are you kidding? We're so close we'll feel their hot, angry breath!"

Lara grimaced, imagining that bull's breath didn't smell all that pleasant. Then, amidst the growing din of the crowd, she sat down and took in the sights.

The arena consisted of an enclosed oblong area that had bucking chutes on one end and a roping chute on the opposite side. The flooring consisted of a clay and sand mixture spread around and loosened with some sort of harrow. Watching the grounds crew finish its final preparations caused Lara to feel bad for Kevin who had been injured somewhere out there. She wondered if he was any better this evening.

"Is this where we're sitting?" a feminine voice asked, although it sounded more like an exclamation.

Shaking herself from her reverie, Lara turned to see her

brother, Tim, and his fiancée, Amanda standing in the aisle.

"This is it," she replied, waving them in. "We're practically in the front row."

"So I see." Tim allowed Amanda to scoot in first. He then sat down on the end of the metallic bench. "Did you and Polly get programs?"

In reply to her brother's question, Lara nodded and held hers up so Tim could see it.

"Kevin Wincouser's part of this rodeo. Remember that guy, Lara? Open your program, and you'll see his picture. Mom said she heard on the news that he got hurt."

Lara laughed at her brother's rapid-fire remarks. "I was at the hospital when Flight brought Kevin in yesterday."

"And you didn't say anything?" Tim appeared insulted.

"I couldn't. There are laws I have to abide by, or I'll lose my job, you know?"

Her brother shrugged.

"But now that the media is reporting Kevin's injury, I don't have to keep it a secret anymore." Lara glanced at her program, knowing she was prohibited from discussing his condition. What the media reported was all she could confirm.

"Wow, Kevin Wincouser. . ." Tim shook his head. "He was like my hero or something."

"Yeah, mine too," Lara admitted, leaning over Polly and Amanda in order to converse with her brother."

"Is this the guy you're talking about?" Amanda asked, pointing at a photo in her program. Her long, straight, platinum blond hair hung past her shoulders, adorned by a simple red plastic headband.

Lara tried not to envy her future sister-in-law's flawless beauty. Bright blue eyes, a trim figure, and gorgeous locks, Amanda Erikson was model material. But what caused her to be so special was that the younger woman was just as attractive on the inside. She had a sweet, caring heart and would do just about anything for anybody.

Tim, a sweetheart himself, was a tall, lanky, brunette. He was the veritable computer geek of the Donahue family, and he had found a gem in Amanda. They made an adorable couple, and Lara was looking forward to their wedding in the fall.

Polly gave Lara a nudge. "Look. There's some activity in the bullpens."

"Bullpens? That's baseball, you nut. What you're staring at are called bucking chutes"

"No, what I'm staring at is a cowboy in a black Stetson heading this way."

Lara whipped her gaze to the left and saw Brent striding toward them. In one smooth move, he jumped up on the side of the stands and clasped the overhead green metal railing. "Glad you could make it," he said with a dashing smile.

Lara returned the gesture, then began introductions. "This is my friend, Polly Nivens."

With his left arm wrapped around the rail, Brent pulled off his tan leather glove and stuck out his right hand. "Pleasure to meet you, Polly."

"Same here." Reaching over Lara, she clasped his hand in a friendly shake.

"And this is my brother, Tim, and his fiancée, Amanda."

Lara watched Brent's expression as he glanced down the row and bobbed out a polite nod. He didn't seem star-struck by Amanda's good looks, which upped Lara's estimation of him.

"Mac heard from the docs at your hospital," Brent said, focusing on Lara. "Apparently they're going to try to wake up Wink on Monday."

"Really? They're bringing out his coma so soon? That's awesome!"

Brent narrowed his brown-eyed gaze. "We'll see."

Lara wondered what he meant but didn't get the opportunity to ask.

"I'd better go. Just wanted to, um, swing by," Brent stated, indicating the railing he still gripped, "and say hello."

Lara and Polly smiled, and Brent tugged on the brim of his hat before jumping off the edge of the bleachers.

"Why didn't you tell me he's drop dead gorgeous?!" Polly shrieked, putting her hands around Lara's neck and giving her a playful shake.

"I did tell you."

Amanda leaned over. "I think I'll buy Tim a Stetson for Christmas. What do you think?"

"Can't turn a frog into a handsome prince," Polly quipped. "Correction—handsome *cowboy*."

Lara frowned. "Hey, that's my brother you're insulting."

"And my fiancée." Amanda raised her perfectly shaped chin in mock indignation.

"Right. You two love him. That's why you need *me* to point out the obvious."

"Amanda, let's both spill our sodas on Polly's lap later, accidentally, of course."

"Not good enough. I think we should volunteer her as a clown during the bull-riding competition tonight."

Lara laughed, Polly smirked, and Amanda wore an expression that said she'd get even—in one amusing way or another.

The rodeo began with a booming overhead announcement that came on so fast it startled Lara. Then, a pre-show commenced with a parade of pretty white horses wearing decorative headpieces. Dancers stood on the animals' backs, performing a variety of acrobatic moves and all to a popular western tune that soon had the audience clapping their hands and singing along.

Once the preceding entertainment ended, the contestants

were introduced. A familiar song played in the background, warning mothers not to let their children grow up to be cowboys.

"Next, and currently in third place, is Brent Yiska."

Lara applauded with the rest of the audience but soon felt Polly lean toward her.

"What kind of name is Yiska?"

"Beats me."

"Polly Yiska. . .has a nice ring to it."

Lara stopped in midclap and gaped at her friend. "Polly Yiska?"

She turned and smiled. "I think I'm in love. I'll never wash my right hand again."

The two started laughing so hard, before long their sides ached.

Then the bull riding began. Contained in the chutes just several feet away, the fierce animals stomped and snorted. Cowboys stood on something that looked like a catwalk on top of one end of the chute. When the rider lowered himself on the bull's back, other cowboys held onto his vest until he nodded, signaling he was ready for the chute to be opened. The bull lunged out, kicking its hind legs and twisting its massive body in one direction, then the other, determined to unseat the man astride it.

Lara found herself tensing and cringing each time a cowboy was bucked off. Even Brent couldn't hang on long enough, and Lara feared he'd be trampled·after he hit the ground. But several clowns immediately appeared to distract the bull, and riders on horseback or "pickup men," according to Tim, showed up to haze the bull out of the ring.

As the rodeo neared its end, Brent stopped by once more, but this time he encouraged all four of them to come back out for tomorrow's events. He offered them another set of passes.

"Thanks. That's really nice of you. But I'm involved with my local church," Lara informed him, "and ministry fills up most of my Sunday."

"Same goes for Amanda and me," Tim said.

Polly sighed. "Me too. . .but I wish I could come back. I had a fun time tonight."

Brent grinned. "That's good." He paused while the ladies collected their purses and Tim gathered their trash. "It's been nice to meet you all, and next time the rodeo's in town, you'll have to come visit again." He turned his head, catching Lara's eye. "I imagine I'll see you at the hospital on Monday."

"It's very possible."

He gave her a parting nod, then bid farewell to the others and returned to wherever it was the cowboys hung out when they weren't competing.

On the way home, Lara and Polly stopped to pick up a pizza, which they planned to eat at Lara's place.

"You're awfully quiet, Polly. Is anything wrong?"

"No. . .not *wrong*. I'm just wrestling with an issue."

"Can you tell me about it?"

"I'd rather not, at least not now. Maybe later."

"All right." Lara didn't push her friend to say more, although she had a feeling the "issue" had something to do with Brent Yiska.

five

"Kevin, can you hear me?"

A commanding male voice penetrated the darkness. Kevin opened his mouth to reply, but it felt as dry as Oklahoma dirt, and all he could do was croak out a vowel sound. He swallowed only to discover his throat was raw and tender. Before he could wonder why, another question came at him.

"Kevin, can you count backwards from ten?"

From beneath some dark, heavy shroud, he began, "Ten, nine, eight, seven, six, five, four, three, two, one. . ."

☙

On Monday morning, Lara could hardly concentrate on her work. The emergency department bustled with sick patients, and tensions ran high. It didn't seem like she'd ever be able to sneak away to the NICU to find out about Kevin.

By midafternoon, she found a few minutes to pull up his name on the computer. Lara discovered he had been transferred to a regular floor, meaning his condition had improved. Rejoicing and thanking the Lord, she went about her work with renewed enthusiasm.

At four-thirty, Lara punched out, feeling the exhaustion weighing on her limbs. The day passed in such a flurry, she hadn't even found time for a lunch break. The second-shift social worker had come in at three and the overlap helped Lara catch up so she could leave work on time.

Now to see how Kevin fared.

Walking around the hospital, using the lower level tunnel that took her past the cafeteria, Lara arrived at the patient elevators and took the car to the fifth floor. She found her way to Kevin's room and met Brent and Mac standing just outside the doorway.

"Well, look who's here. The little social worker."

Lara forced a smile in Mac's direction, despite the woman's sarcastic greeting. She looked at Brent, hoping for an ally. "I came up to see how Kevin's doing."

"Not so good," he replied in a tight voice. "He doesn't remember any of us."

"After all I've done for him," Mac muttered.

"You got paid for all you did." Brent slid an annoyed look in Mac's direction.

"Maybe Kevin's memory lapse is only temporary." Lara glanced between the two, then back to Brent. "What do the doctors say?"

"Don't know. Haven't seen 'em."

"If you'd like, I can ask the unit secretary to page the doctor on call."

"Yeah, maybe. . ."

"I'll ask her." Mac pushed past Lara in a huff.

"Don't mind her," Brent said. "She feels a little insulted. I s'pose we all do. We've been Wink's friends for years—we've been more than friends. We're like family."

"What about Kevin's brother? I meant to ask all weekend if he'd been contacted."

"Wink has a brother?" Brent's brown eyes widened in surprise. "I never knew that. Maybe you've got the wrong Kevin Wincouser after all."

"Hmm. . ." Lara didn't think so. But at the same time, she wondered why his good friends, his family, didn't know about Clayt.

Leaning forward, she peeked into Kevin's room.

"Go on in," Brent drawled. "He's kinda groggy, but he's

awake. Quincy's in there along with Jimmy."

Lara glanced at Brent, acknowledging his reply with a nod. Then she slowly stepped up to Kevin's bedside. It heartened her to see him without all the tubes and the ventilator from Friday night. She smiled a quick greeting to Quincy the Clown and the young cowboy. The two men sat in chairs near the window.

Looking back at Kevin, Lara touched his arm. She spoke his name, and he blinked.

"Don't expect too much," Lara heard Brent say as he came to stand beside her.

"I don't." She tried again. "Kevin?"

His lids fluttered open, revealing startling blue eyes that Lara thought she'd know anywhere. She'd dreamed of those eyes hundreds of times.

She smiled. "Hi, Kevin."

His gaze lingered on her face for a long moment, and then a grin pulled at the corner his parched-looking lips. He closed his eyes. "Lara Donahue. You're a. . .a sight for sore eyes."

Her smile widened. "You remember me?"

"Sure." He looked at her again before his lids dropped closed, as if they were too heavy for him to keep open. "You've changed a little."

"A little? Since my sophomore year of high school? I would hope that I've changed a lot." She laughed and noticed a hint of an amused expression on Kevin's face.

"How's. . .family. . .parents? Ruth and Timmy?"

"Everyone's fine. Dad just retired, but Mom still teaches part-time at the grade school. Ruth is married with three kids, and Tim is getting married this fall."

"You married? Kids?" He asked the question with his eyes closed, and his words sounded slurred, probably from any number of medications Kevin was being given.

"No husband," Lara teased, "but I have kids. About twelve last time I counted."

Brent shifted his stance and now regarded her with a look of shock. "You're kidding. You? Twelve kids?"

"Yep."

"No way!"

Lara looked back at Kevin and saw that his chapped lips had split into a grin. "Lara, you're a. . .a terrible liar."

"You're right. But I really do have twelve kids. I volunteer at The Regeneration Ranch. It's a place where physically challenged children can learn to ride horses. And I can do that, Kevin, because you taught me how to ride."

"I remember. . ."

So did Lara, and she suddenly felt like she had a crush on him all over again.

Brent sat down on the end of Kevin's bed. "I should have known you didn't really have twelve kids—of your own, I mean."

"No, not of my own." Smiling, Lara focused on the patient. "So, um, Kev," she said, using his childhood nickname, "you're kind of banged up."

"Yeah, that's what they say."

"Do you remember how it happened?"

"No. . ."

Mac walked into the room, and Brent relayed the news. "Wink knows her. That's a good sign."

"Sure is," said Quincy, wearing an ear-to-ear grin.

Mac only scowled at Lara.

Tamping down the intimidation she felt around the snarly woman, she looked at Kevin only to find him staring back at her.

"Who are these people?"

"They're your friends."

Brent stood and leaned on the bed's guardrail. "I'm your

best friend, Wink. You don't remember me?"

"You *were* his best friend," Mac added with a snide grin, "until he stole your girl right from under your nose."

Lara widened her eyes at the remark. "Kevin would never do that!"

Brent straightened and pursed his lips, regarding Kevin all the while. "Sure he would. . .and he did."

Kevin stared back, his blue-eyed gaze obviously drawing a blank. Lara realized in that moment that she didn't know this man anymore.

"Well, listen," Brent drawled, "it doesn't matter. Emily wasn't worth my time anyhow."

"You can say that again," Jimmy interjected.

The stress level in the room suddenly skyrocketed, and Lara felt like she was about to break out in a cold sweat.

Kevin reached out, took hold of her forearm, and Lara decided that, for an invalid, he had a strong grip as he pulled her nearer to him.

"Lara, you've got to help me," he whispered. "I feel like I'm in a nightmare."

Her heart ached for him. "It's okay. Don't worry. Just rest, all right?" She placed her free hand over his. "Things will get better as you recuperate."

She saw doubt flicker in his eyes, and she gave him a reassuring smile.

"It'll be all right," she repeated. "Go back to sleep and get some rest."

He let his eyes drift shut.

Lara slid her arm out from beneath his grasp and noticed the eerie silence that had crept into the room.

Finally, Brent dispelled it when he blew out an audible sigh. "I hope I'm never in such sad shape that a woman has to fawn all over me that way."

Lara grew embarrassed for a second time. "I didn't mean to 'fawn,' as you put it. Kevin is a longtime friend, that's all."

She saw Mac roll her eyes but not before she glimpsed the mischievous expression on Brent's face.

"What kind of *longtime friend*?" he asked.

"Not like you're thinking," she retorted.

Brent chuckled. "So now you can read my mind, huh?"

Lara changed the subject. She disliked sparring with this man, mostly because she was afraid she'd lose. "Say, can I treat you all to dinner in the cafeteria? I didn't get lunch, so I'm starved, and today's special is one of my favorites. Homemade gyros."

"I'm game," Jimmy stated.

"You're always game when there's food involved," Mac muttered.

Quincy rose from his chair. "Well, I sure could use some supper."

"Not me," Mac said. "I have work to do. I'll see you boys back at the fairgrounds."

Lara tried not to look relieved when the petite redhead in snug blue jeans marched out of the room.

"Gyros sound okay," Brent said. "You're on, Miss Lara, the social worker."

She smiled, a gesture that belied her sudden awkward feelings.

Suddenly, she thought of Polly and decided to call and invite her. "My friend works a split shift, and it's about time for her dinner break. I'm going to give her a quick call."

Using the phone on the side table, Lara lifted its receiver and dialed the NICU's extension.

"Hey, Pol, I'm taking Kevin's friends, Quincy, Jimmy, and Brent, to the cafeteria for dinner. Want to come along?"

"Brent's there?"

"Uh-huh." Lara forced herself not to glance over her shoulder at him.

"Oh, wow, is it my lucky day or what? Sure, I'll come. I'll meet you in the cafeteria."

"Great. See you in a few minutes."

Grinning, Lara hung up the phone, and her odd uneasiness waned. Then she recalled her friend's comment on Saturday night—"Polly Yiska. . .has a nice ring to it"—and Lara had to stifle her amusement.

Polly Yiska indeed!

Lara paused by Kevin's bedside, touched the back of his hand, and sent up another prayer for God's healing. Moments later, she left the room and caught up to his friends already in the hallway and nearing the elevators. She told herself Kevin's memory loss wasn't anything to fret about. God could do anything!

six

Traumatic brain injury. Those three words struck terror into Kevin's soul. He wanted to believe this was some sort of bad dream. However, the weakness he felt on his right side as the doctor maneuvered his limbs was all too real. Still, he listened to the neurologist explain the injuries and talk of extensive rehabilitation.

"What about his memory loss?"

Startled by the soft, feminine voice, Kevin glanced to his left and saw Lara Donahue standing at his bedside. When had she appeared, and how was she involved in all this? Maybe this was some crazy nightmare after all. He hadn't thought about Lara Donahue in. . .well, in half of forever.

He stared at her, noticing the look of concern in her hazel eyes. Her honey-colored hair with its blond streaks had been combed back and clipped. However, feathery bangs covered Lara's forehead. She looked professional. Of course, the dark green suit she wore only added to that upper-management image, and Kevin decided the plump, ugly duckling he'd known in high school had definitely turned into a lovely swan with curves in just the right places.

He sighed with relief. At least *that* part of his brain hadn't been damaged.

Closing his eyes, Kevin fought the grogginess that dogged him. He realized he was drifting in and out of consciousness and missing portions of the conversation.

"Short-term memory loss is actually quite common in this sort of situation," he heard the doctor say. The man had a

46

dark complexion and a thick accent. Kevin wondered where the guy was from. . .India, perhaps. "I think he will get his memory back in a day or so."

"What if he doesn't?"

Kevin opened his eyes to see the same three men who had been in his room earlier standing next to Lara. The one who asked the question claimed to be Kevin's "best friend."

"We cannot deal with the 'what ifs' at this time," the wiry doctor stated, setting Kevin's right arm back onto the sheet-covered mattress and pulling the light blue coverlet over the top of his body. "For now, we're glad that he's conscious and that he can speak because it means he's processing information. All very good signs so far. We will have to take things one day at a time. Okay?"

Kevin grinned at the way the man's voice went up an octave when he said, "okay." Then he followed the doctor out of the room with his gaze before looking at Lara.

She smiled at him. "Pretty good news, Kev."

He had so many questions. "Why are you here?"

"Me?" She appeared taken aback. "Don't you want me here? I'm sorry. I can leave—"

"No, that's. . .not what I meant." It was an effort to form even the simplest of words. When he finally managed it, they sounded as if he'd consumed two six-packs of beer.

His head sort of felt like he'd been drinking too.

"Lara, I haven't seen you in. . .ages. What. . .what are you doing here?"

"Oh." She smiled. "I work here. I'm a social worker." Her voice had that same happy lilt as when they were kids, and somehow it made Kevin feel like everything might really be all right. "I was part of the Trauma Team on duty when Flight-for-Life brought you in. I recognized your name and. . .well, I hope you don't mind that I involved myself in your case."

"I don't mind."

"My parents and Tim heard about your accident on the news. They want to come and see you. Is that okay?"

"Sure."

"I told them tomorrow night might be better, since you just got out of the NICU today."

"I imagine I'll be here."

"Well, we won't." The cowboy with the reddish brown hair sat down on the end of his bed. "We're all hitting the road tomorrow morning."

"Where to?"

"South Dakota and the Cyprus Ranch Rodeo."

The name lit a spark in Kevin, and he knew he had to be there. "I'll catch up."

"Now, Wink, the doctor said you've got months of rehab ahead of you." Kevin watched as an older man stepped around his bedside. He looked familiar. And an image of a clown flashed across his mind. "Didn't you hear what that doctor said?"

"I know you," Kevin managed. "Quincy. Quincy Owens."

The older man let out a whoop that ping-ponged off all four walls of his hospital room. "Your memory's comin' back, Wink. That's great." Quincy placed a wide hand on Kevin's shoulder. "That's just great."

Kevin did his best to grin at the man who had been a father figure to him the past nine years.

"Do you remember me now?" asked a fresh-faced kid with a buzzed hairstyle.

Kevin studied his facial features but drew a blank. He looked at the other man, his "best friend," but again, he couldn't recall a name or how he knew him.

"No. . .not yet."

"It'll come," Lara said.

"Just don't strain yourself, Wink," the other cowboy said,

narrowing his brown eyes. "Weren't too many brain cells in your head to begin with."

The younger man laughed, and Quincy told them both to have a little decency.

"Can't you see Wink's hurtin' right now?"

Kevin couldn't suppress the grin that reached his lips, and as he regarded his supposed best friend, intuition told him he'd met his match—in more ways than one.

❧

"So tell me everything you know about rodeos."

Sitting outside on the second-story porch of her parents' home with Polly, Lara laughed. "I know about as much as you do."

"No, you know more. You knew what a bucking chute was. Please. . .I want to be able to talk to Brent about something."

"You might start by talking to him about Jesus."

"I will. Whenever I get a chance."

"Sorry to say, but I don't think you'll get that chance."

"How do you know?"

"He's leaving tomorrow morning. I think you should just forget about Brent Yiska."

Lara lifted her long legs, planting the heels of her bare feet on the porch railing. Tonight as they had dined in County General's cafeteria, it seemed to Lara as though Brent purposely tried to catch her eye. In a word, flirt. Once she realized it, she tried not to glance in his direction as he sat catercorner from her across the long table. The whole scene had made Lara feel uncomfortable, especially since Polly appeared to be hopelessly infatuated with the handsome cowboy.

"He's too charming for his own good," Lara told her friend. "He's a lady's man."

"Are you interested in him?"

"Me? No!" Realizing her reply sounded overly enthusiastic,

she calmed her voice, adding, "I want a man who's walking with the Lord, someone who will care about my spiritual well-being."

"You don't know that Brent's *not* a Christian."

"True. He's a nice enough person, and I've never heard him curse. He's never given me a reason to think he isn't a believer. But, Polly, you know me. I would rather err on the side of caution than get emotionally involved with a man who doesn't share my beliefs."

"I know, I know. . .and I feel the same way." She paused for a long moment. "Lara, this is going to sound insane, but when I first set eyes on Brent, it's like God said, 'That's him.'?"

"Are you sure it was God?"

"Positive. Who else speaks to my heart like that?"

Lara shrugged. Leaning her head back, she gazed up at the dusky sky. A soft breeze rustled the treetops that canopied the Donahue's front yard.

"Whenever I imagined myself married to someone, I imagined. . .Brent and everything about him. His dark brown hair and somewhat cynical brown eyes, broad shoulders—"

"Okay, okay. Spare me the details."

"You don't like him?"

"It's not that, Polly. Brent seems nice. But he's a. . .a *player*."

"You really think so?"

"Yep."

Polly grew quiet, obviously thinking everything over. Silence filled the space between them, except for some chirping birds in one of the nearby treetops.

"Do you think Brent is worse than Bob Robinson?"

Lara deliberated, recalling the last time she'd seen Bob at one of the Christian singles' functions. "No one is worse than that dude."

"Good, he's got one up on Bob, anyway."

Lara laughed.

Just then, Tim burst through the screen door and stepped onto the porch. "Hey, look what I printed off the Internet. It's the PRCA's unofficial standings as of yesterday. Brent's in third place in bull riding with nine thousand two hundred thirty-six points. Kevin slipped to seventh place in bareback riding, but there's an article about his accident and a couple of pictures."

Tim handed the pages to Lara. She glanced over the information before handing them to Polly.

"What's PRCA stand for?" Polly wanted to know.

"Professional Rodeo Cowboys Association," Tim informed her.

"Boy, do I have a lot to learn."

Lara grinned and looked at her brother. "Kevin said you could visit him tomorrow evening."

"Oh, great, I'll plan on stopping at the hospital after work. Mom said Kevin is doing better today."

Lara nodded. "Yes, but one of the residents told me that he'll be surprised if Kevin ever returns to the rodeo circuit." Her heart broke for him, and she wondered how he'd take the news.

"Well, you never know," Tim said. "Doctors have been wrong before."

"That's true." Lara stood. "I'm going to make some popcorn. Be right back."

As she walked through the living room and into the kitchen where her grandmother stood at the sink, peeling an apple, Lara prayed that Kevin would make a full recovery. The rodeo had obviously been his whole life for the past ten years—and even before that. Kevin was always involved in the statewide junior rodeos in high school. As Lara recalled, he always did well. It didn't surprise her that Kevin was a two-time world bareback champion.

Suddenly, she remembered Brent's claim that Kevin had stolen his "girl." Was it true? If so, what sort of life had Kevin been living?

He's a Christian. Things happen like that. . .even to believers. Besides, it is none of my business.

"You're deep in thought, Muffin," Gram said.

Lara extracted herself from her musings. "Yeah. . .just thinking about Kevin."

"Doing a lot of that lately."

"More than I should."

"Well, you were awfully fond of that boy," Gram said with a knowing twinkle in her rheumy eyes. "Maybe you still are."

"No, Gram." Lara chuckled. The insinuation sounded as foolish as Polly hearing God tell her that Brent Yiska was "The One."

Nevertheless, deep in her heart of hearts, a question sparked. Lara quickly extinguished it. She wasn't about to get emotionally involved with one of her patients. True, Kevin was a childhood friend, but it was also true that she had a job to do, and Lara took it seriously.

Shaking off Gram's implication, Lara flung a package of unpopped corn into the microwave, punched in the time, and waited for it to cook.

seven

"I came to say good-bye."

Kevin stared at the woman hanging over his bedside. For the life of him, he couldn't remember who she was. She did look familiar. . .but probably because she'd been in his room yesterday with Quincy and the other two cowboys. Kevin had also concluded that she was a redheaded spitfire with a tongue so sharp it could shred a man in seconds flat. He'd seen her rip apart that younger guy named Jimmy after he'd made some inane remark.

"I'll miss you, but I have to get back to Houston," she said in a sultry tone. "Daddy's expecting me."

"Okay." Kevin didn't know what else to say. With no one else in the room, he felt vulnerable, defenseless. Only one word described this woman—scary. He wished a nurse would walk in right about now and take his vitals. Give him a shot. Anything.

Taking a deep breath, she leaned closer. Kevin smelled her heavy perfume, and it made the bridge of his nose ache. "Of course, Daddy's upset about your accident. It'll cost the company millions. But I've got a plan. We'll play up your injuries, get some magazines to write your story, and once you return to the rodeo, you'll be a hero. . .and so will we for standing by your side through thick and thin."

"What company?" Kevin felt more confused than ever.

The woman straightened and gave him a glare. "Sabino's Authentic Mexican Foods, of course. You must remember. We're the leading brand of salsa, con queso, hot sauce, and bean dips." She heaved an impatient sigh. "Come on, Wink."

"Sabino's. . .yeah. . ." He'd heard the name before.

"We're your sponsor."

Kevin might not remember much, but he knew that cowboys needed their sponsors.

"But don't worry," she said, turning on her velveteen voice again, "I'll soothe Daddy's ruffled feathers."

"Well, thanks."

Seeing the smile curve her red-painted lips, Kevin gave her a polite grin.

Then, in a flash, she put her hands on either side of his face and brought her mouth to his, in a devouring kiss. She might have even crawled into his hospital bed, had Kevin not pushed her back with his left hand.

"Whoa," he said, catching his breath. "What do you think you're doing?"

"I love you, Wink. Tell me you love me too. Say we'll get married just as soon as you're out of this horrible place."

Kevin opened his mouth to inform her that he didn't even know her name, let alone love her.

"Better yet, let's transfer you to Houston's medical center so I can keep my eye on you."

Kevin knew he didn't want that.

"Say you love me."

"I–I. . ."

"Yes? Say it, Wink."

"What are you wantin' him to say, Mac?"

Kevin swung his gaze to the doorway and sighed with relief seeing Quincy standing there.

"I told you I needed some time alone with Wink," the woman spat. "What are you doing here?"

Quincy stepped forward, met Kevin's gaze, and shook his head. "You've got lipstick all over your face, Son."

Taking the small Kleenex box off the rollaway tray, he tossed it at Kevin who caught it with his strong hand. Pulling out several tissues, he proceeded to wipe his mouth.

"You're nothing but a meddling old man," Mac spat, making her way around Kevin's bed. "You're a has-been bull rider reduced to being a clown people laugh at—even when you're not made up and dressed in your ridiculous outfits."

"Hey!" Kevin felt defensive for his friend. He tried to sit up, but Quincy placed his hands on his shoulders and held him back.

"You need to stay still, Boy."

Mac had long since stomped out of the room.

"Whoo-whee, that woman has a wicked tongue." Kevin felt suddenly exhausted after the encounter. "Who is she?"

Quincy grinned. He seemed unaffected by the insults flung at him only moments before. "That's Mackenzie Sabino. Her father is owner and CEO of Sabino's, your sponsor. Mac has followed your career for years. She's a regular rodeo groupie and tells everyone that she's in love with you."

"Do I love her back?"

"I sure hope not, otherwise I'll have to give you another head injury."

Kevin laughed, causing his temples to throb. "Oh, man, I think my pain medicine is wearing off."

"Want me to get the nurse?"

"Yeah, would you?"

"Sure, and I think Miss Lara was on her way in to see you. I met her by the elevators. Maybe she saw Mac kissing you and decided you were *indisposed*."

"Oh, no. . ." Kevin rolled his head toward the windows. The blinds were partially open, allowing in a sprinkling of morning sunshine.

"What's wrong?"

He looked back at Quincy. "When we were kids, Lara thought the world of me, and well, I know this sounds odd considering my track record with women, but I don't want Lara's opinion of me to slip because of that. . .that red-headed vixen."

Quincy hooted. "You're right. It does sound odd coming from you. You're a regular Casanova. Won't be long, and you'll have every female nurse on this floor fawning all over you. But, if it'll make you feel any better, I'll stop by on my way out and tell Miss Lara what really happened up here."

"Yeah. . ." Kevin disliked Quincy's character description, even though he knew it was true. "Yeah, will you straighten Lara out for me?"

"Will do."

❧

Lara felt troubled and distracted when she returned to her office. With the ED relatively quiet, she'd made the trek to the fifth floor to say good morning to Kevin. Unfortunately for her, she'd walked in on a love scene that wasn't exactly PG-13.

In her mind's eye, she could still see Mac plastered against Kevin's chest, her delicate hands with their long, red, manicured fingernails caressing his face. Kevin had placed his left hand on Mac's shoulder, and Lara imagined he drew Mac nearer to him. Obviously, the two of them were involved in a serious relationship. Kevin must have suddenly remembered Mac, and perhaps the intimate exchange was their way of celebrating.

Lara tamped down her jealous feelings. Where had they come from anyway? *Probably Gram and all her teasing about my schoolgirl crush on Kevin. . .*

Doing her best to dismiss the less-than-professional thoughts from her mind, Lara tucked her portfolio under her arm and headed into the ER. At the physician's request, she entered a patient's room and began an amicable conversation that soon became a lengthy interview. Lara discovered the young woman named Amber was three months pregnant and wanted help with her drug addiction. Lara scheduled an appointment for her, then supplied Amber with a bus ticket, courtesy of County General, so she'd have transportation to the treatment center.

"Thanks," Amber said with a shaky smile. Her complexion looked so pale, it seemed almost transparent.

"You're welcome. Call me and let me know how you're doing." Lara held out one of her business cards. After accepting it, Amber gave her a hug.

Feeling satisfied to have helped someone, Lara returned to her office. She sent up a prayer for Amber, asking the Lord, somehow, to reach the young lady during this crisis. Sitting down at her desk, Lara begun to make some notes, and then her pager sounded. She dialed the extension illuminated on the device's tiny screen and was informed by a registrar in the front lobby that someone was waiting to speak with her.

Gathering her portfolio once more, Lara left her office. When she entered the lobby and saw Quincy chatting with the security guard near the front doors, she hid her surprise.

"I thought you'd be long gone by now," she said walking toward him.

"Couldn't leave town without saying *adios* to Wink."

Lara replied with a tight smile.

"I also wanted to thank you for being so kind to Jimmy, Brent, and me. Mac too."

"Just doing my job."

Quincy narrowed his gaze, and Lara looked away, glancing down at the end of the lobby where a tall African-American man dropped coins into one of the vending machines.

"You're upset, aren't you? Wink thought you might think badly of him, so he asked me to explain. See, what you saw up there—"

Lara touched her forefinger to her lips, silencing Quincy. The last thing she wanted was to become the subject of gossip, and judging from the security guard's interested expression, he was all ears. "Why don't we discuss this in my office?"

"Good idea."

Lara led the way back to her cramped work area at the far end of the emergency department.

"It's cozy," Quincy said.

Lara laughed. "That's a nice way of describing my. . .*cubbyhole*. It's not even mine, either. I have to share it with two other social workers."

Quincy chuckled and lowered himself into one of the two armchairs near her desk. "Now about Mac. . ."

Lara held up a hand. "You really don't have to explain. Kevin's personal life isn't any of my business. I involved myself in his case because we knew each other as kids."

"Well, since you're involved now, you need to know that Mac throws herself at Wink anytime she sees an opportunity. She's like gum on his shoe, and Wink's gotta be nice to her because her father owns the company that sponsors him. Making the gum even stickier is the fact that Mac convinced her daddy to invest more money in Wink and promote his career with the idea that the more famous he gets, the more money Sabino's will make. Personally, I believe Mac thinks if she has a hand in furthering Wink's career, he'll marry her. Little does she know that Wink's not the marrying kind."

Lara sent him a polite smile. She wondered if Quincy was trying to warn her in some roundabout way. But, of course, there was no need for cautionary words. "Look, it's true that I do care about Kevin more than if he was a regular patient here at County General. Our parents attended the same dinner parties, and the Wincousers went to our church. But that's the extent of it."

"You told me all that, and it's understandable why you'd take a special interest in Wink. That was clear from day one—or maybe day two."

Lara's smile broadened. "I love people in general. That's why I went into this profession."

"And that's about as obvious as a bull in a teashop. I'm not concerned," Quincy said with a hint of smirk. "Wink sent me here because he didn't want your opinion of him to lessen. . .you know, since you happened to walk into his room during that latest *Mac Attack*."

Lara laughed. "Mac Attack?"

"Yeah, that's what me and the boys have taken to calling those. . .um. . .incidents."

"I see." Another giggle escaped before Lara could stop it.

"But the good news is Mac's flying home to Houston today, although I doubt that's the end of her."

"I appreciate that bit of warning."

"Yep, I thought you might." Quincy stood to his feet. He wore a black cotton shirt with silver buttons and black jeans. A rather dark outfit, Lara decided, for a guy employed as a rodeo clown. Regardless, he was a likeable fellow.

"Quincy, it's been a pleasure to meet you." Lara stuck out her right hand, and he gave it a firm shake.

"Likewise. We'll check in with Wink every couple of days. We drive from here to South Dakota for this next weekend's rodeo. The summer schedule is intense."

"I understand." Lara escorted Quincy to the lobby.

"It's a blessing you're here, Miss Lara," he drawled. "At least we're not leaving Wink in the hands of complete strangers, bad enough we've got to leave him at all."

Lara caught the word "blessing," and it piqued her curiosity. "Quincy, are you a Christian?"

He paused. "I have my own faith."

She sensed no open door, so she didn't pursue the matter. "Um, I see." She smiled. "Again, it was really nice to meet you."

Quincy's guarded expression crumbled, and he smiled. "Nice to meet you too." He took a few steps forward, then paused. "Oh, and. . .I got the impression your friend Polly's set her cap for Brent."

"It's that obvious, eh?"

"Sure is. But she should know that he's not the marrying kind, either."

"I suspected as much, and I tried to warn her. Polly wouldn't listen."

"Tell her again." Quincy grinned. "Both he and Wink learned from my mistakes. I made 'em swear they wouldn't follow in my footsteps."

"Oh?" Lara tipped her head, curious.

"Yep. I was married three times, and I can honestly say there's no such thing as wedded bliss."

"Talk to my parents about that subject," Lara countered. "They've been married for thirty-five years."

A frown crinkled Quincy's brow. "I'm referring to happiness."

"So am I." He seemed to weigh her reply before giving her a friendly smile. "Well, there's always an exception, isn't there?" He chuckled, then continued the trek into the lobby.

Lara watched him go, thinking how sad it was that Quincy thought "for better or for worse" was an exception. To her, marriage vows meant forever, and for herself, Lara wouldn't consider anything less.

eight

Lara debated whether to stop in and see Kevin before leaving work. Her parents, Tim, and Amanda were planning to visit, so he wouldn't be without company, and Lara felt exhausted. She wanted nothing more than to go home, change clothes, eat supper, and watch a few mindless television programs. But she surmised that, by not stopping in after Quincy made a point to explain about the "Mac Attack" this morning, Kevin might think she was disappointed in him or worse. The truth was, Lara couldn't have cared less. At least she kept telling herself that.

Riding the elevator to the fifth floor, Lara exited and made her way to Kevin's room. She walked in and immediately spotted all the flowers lining the wide window ledge. Glancing at Kevin, she saw that he slept despite the noise from the TV hanging up in the corner.

Lara strode to his bedside, located the controls, and muted the local newscast so it wouldn't disturb Kevin. She noted the steady rise and fall of his broad chest, then her gaze moved upward to his shadowy jaw. The small cleft in his chin was still visible through the stubble. Without intending to, Lara found herself studying the perfect shape of his mouth, and after remembering this morning's passionate scene, Lara wondered what it would feel like to be the recipient of Kevin's kisses.

What am I thinking? I must be deranged!

Glancing at the flowers again, she steadied her thoughts. But when she looked back at Kevin, she discovered his blue eyes staring at her.

"Lara," he said sounding groggy. "I'm sorry. Did I fall asleep while you were talking?"

Her cheeks burned with embarrassment. She hadn't meant to ogle him while he lay sleeping—and now he'd caught her at it!

"I–I wasn't saying anything. I just came up to see how you're doing."

"You're a sweetheart, Lara. You've always been a sweet-heart."

"Oh, I don't know about that." She glanced down at her hands, resting on the metal guardrail.

"Well, I do. You always rushed to the aid of someone in need." Kevin's words came out in slow succession, as if it took a great effort to form each one. "You were like the little mother of the neighborhood, taking care of everybody, running to the grocery store for the old ladies, comforting little kids who fell off their bikes. That's the Lara Donahue I remember."

Lara grinned. "I tried. I guess I wanted people to like me since most of my peers made fun of me because I was fat."

"Kids can be mean."

"You and Clayt were never mean. Your parents raised you right, that's for sure."

Kevin's blue eyes widened, and an anguished expression washed across his face.

"Did I say something wrong? I'm sorry."

Kevin blinked back whatever emotion had momentarily gripped him. "That's okay. I'll be fine."

"Are you in pain? Should I get your nurse?"

Kevin didn't reply, and Lara began to worry. Was this some reaction to medication? Was something occurring because of his head injury?

She put her hand on his forearm. "Kevin?"

He stared straight ahead, looking across the room at nothing.

"Kevin, please tell me what's wrong."

His gaze inched its way to the left until it reached hers. "I haven't seen or talked to my brother in nine long years."

Lara raised her brows at the unexpected reply. "Oh—"

Kevin bent his arm at the elbow and clasped her hand. "We had a big fight the second Christmas after Mom and Dad were killed. I didn't feel much like celebrating. I hadn't planned on staying through the holiday. That made my aunt and uncle mad. Then, when I told Clayt I just wanted my half of our parents' estate so I could be on my way and live my own life, things got really nasty. In the end, I had to hire an attorney to get what was rightfully mine. You see, my aunt and uncle were control freaks. Still are, as far as I know."

"I'm so sorry, Kev."

"Why are you apologizing?" He gave her hand a squeeze. "Not your fault."

"I'm sorry for you—that you've been estranged from your brother. That's sad. You're flesh and blood. Family."

"The only family I need is my rodeo family. But I could use all the friends I can get." He paused and searched her face. "Will you be my friend, Lara?"

"Of course." She smiled into his deep blue eyes. "You won me over in junior high by being nice to me and teaching me how to ride. I'll always be your friend, Kev."

❧

As the week progressed, Lara made a point to visit Kevin every day on her lunch breaks and after work. Her parents, Gram, and Tim stopped at the hospital twice to say hello, and Kevin remembered them. Lara noticed he enjoyed reminiscing—to a point. However, when the subject touched on his brother Clayt, their deceased parents, or the Lord, Kevin grew quiet, his discomfort evidenced by his silence. The Donahues, out of politeness, changed the topic of discussion.

Then, on Thursday, Mackenzie Sabino called, insisting that Kevin be transferred to a facility in Houston. But when Lara presented him with the option, Kevin refused it.

"My rodeo family is traveling," he said, still sounding groggy, "so I might as well stay put. This hospital is as good as any, I imagine."

Lara relayed Kevin's decision to Mac, and the woman put up such a fuss that Lara was forced to involve the Patient Relations department. They managed to deter the unrelenting Texas belle, but Lara figured it wouldn't be for long.

And it's none of my business, she reminded herself on Friday night as she changed clothes. Tonight marked the monthly Christian singles' group dinner, and neither she nor Polly felt like attending. Lara grinned as she recalled Polly's suggestion for their weekend plans. She wanted to drive to South Dakota to watch Brent in the bull-riding competition.

"By the time we get there, you nut," Lara had replied, "we'll have to turn around and come home."

"It can't take that long to drive to South Dakota. . ."

The telephone rang, startling Lara out of her thoughts. Walking to the other side of her bedroom, she lifted the portable phone and pressed the *TALK* button.

"Hey, it's me."

Lara smiled, hearing Polly's voice. "Hi. What's up?"

"I'm getting bold in my old age."

Lara laughed. Polly was only twenty-six. "What did you do?"

"I called the Cyprus Ranch and left a message for Brent. He called me back."

"How did you manage that? You're still at work." Lara recalled all the many times Polly showed up late at their singles' dinner because her shift ran from eleven in the morning to seven-thirty. Polly worked what was called a "split shift."

"I took a break and used my cell phone, and Brent called

me back in the unit. We're really slow tonight. Only three patients up here. Anyway. . .I told him you and I were looking for something to do this week and that we thought about making the drive to South Dakota. Brent said it wasn't much more than ten hours from Milwaukee, and he sounded pleased that we wanted to come. He also mentioned that he's got some of Wink's things he'd like to send back with us. So, what do you say? If you can't do it for me, do it for Kevin."

Lara rolled her eyes. "Nice try."

"No, listen. Seriously. I figure I can get home, throw some stuff into a suitcase, and pick you up by nine tonight. We'll get to South Dakota by seven tomorrow morning. We'll check into a hotel, sleep until about one o'clock, then head over to the rodeo. It doesn't start until eight at night, but——"

"But you'd like to get some time to talk to Brent."

Polly gasped. "Why, Lara, you read my mind."

"You're crazy!" She laughed as the words tumbled out of her mouth.

"Lara, we never do anything exciting. It's the same thing all the time. Let's live a little. Let's do something impulsive for once."

"Impulsive can be dangerous. Besides, I already told you what Quincy said about Brent. He's not the marrying kind, not to mention he might not even be a believer."

"The same is true about Kevin. You told me that too."

Lara frowned. "What's Kevin got to do with anything?"

"You are as hung up on Kevin as I am on Brent. Admit it."

"No, I won't *admit it* because it's not true."

"Yes it is. You never got over your eighth-grade crush on him."

Lara clenched her jaw, feeling defensive. She opened her mouth to lash out at her friend for stating such untruths but caught herself just in time.

Collecting herself, she said, "If I'm acting like I still have a crush on Kevin, then I need to adjust my behavior."

"Why?"

"Because. . .I'm a professional."

"You're a woman. . .and he used to be a friend."

He is my friend, Lara thought. At least, she'd promised to always be his friend.

Polly sighed. "Look, we'll have ten hours to hash this out. Be ready at nine." With that, she disconnected the call.

Lara's jaw dropped, and she stared at the telephone as if it suddenly grown horns—bull's horns, to be exact.

I can't believe I'm going to do this. But I am!

Walking to her bedroom door, Lara opened it and sauntered into the living room where her grandmother was watching television and crocheting a gorgeous afghan for Tim and Amanda.

"What's the matter, Muffin? You look like you just lost your best friend."

"No, Gram, I'm okay. I just came to tell you that, well, that I'm driving with Polly to South Dakota for the weekend. We're going to another rodeo."

nine

Kevin stared at the white porous ceiling tiles as he lay in his hospital bed. He had a phone number whirling around his mind, but no clue as to whom it belonged. Feeling more cognizant than he had in days, Kevin lifted the phone off the rolling table and placed it on his abdomen. Then, with his left hand, since his right still felt a little more than useless, he pressed in the number and brought the receiver to his ear. It rang at the other end twice, then a familiar male voice answered.

"Hey, it's Wink. Who's this?"

"Well, hey yourself. It's Brent."

A memory flashed across Kevin's mind. A bull rider. His dark brown chaps flinging outward with each kick of the animal's hind legs.

"Brent."

"You remember me yet?"

"Sure do." Kevin realized he'd been here at the hospital with Quincy.

Then another image. A woman with golden blond hair and lying blue eyes. Emily.

"She wasn't good enough for you."

"What? Wink, what are you talking about?"

"Em. Every time you turned your back, she was giving me calf eyes. One night I gave in to her just to prove to you that she wasn't what you thought."

"I don't want to talk about it."

"She ain't worth bustin' up our friendship," Kevin drawled, "that's for sure."

"You feeling better?"

"Sort of." Kevin realized Brent had changed the subject on purpose. "The doctors still have me pretty doped up. They don't want me moving around and injuring my brain worse than it is."

"How would they tell if that happened?" Brent chuckled. "You've been falling on your head for the last decade."

Kevin smirked, figuring half of Brent's remark was probably true. How much could a head take, anyhow?

"So guess who's coming to see me this weekend?"

"Who?"

"Lara the sweet social worker and her friend."

The news surprised Kevin. "Where are you?"

"South Dakota."

Kevin still remembered his geography. "What does Lara want to travel all that way for?"

"Guess I'm worth it."

Kevin could hear the animosity in Brent's voice. Obviously, he wasn't over Em yet. But did he think he could use Lara as payback? Kevin failed to see how that plan would unfold since he had no romantic designs on Lara, but he hoped he was wrong. Lara didn't deserve to get caught in the middle of this skirmish.

"A couple of things you'd best know about her," Kevin began, suddenly feeling exhausted. "One, she's a born-again Christian, and two, she's a package deal, comes with an entire family, including an overprotective father. So consider yourself fairly warned."

"Don't worry about me. But do you think you can live without that woman fawning all over you? It was a pitiful sight if I ever saw one."

Kevin grinned. "Yeah, you're just jealous."

"Oh, right. I sure wish I was lying in a hospital bed, losing points and money, not to mention my standing."

The dig struck the core of Kevin's being. While part of him figured that Brent was still sore about his two-timing girlfriend, another part of Kevin sensed his friend was taking his cutting comment and going for the jugular. Maybe their friendship had already been irreparably damaged.

"Time to hang up," Kevin said, trying to keep his emotions in check. "You have fun this weekend."

He hung up the phone, and for the first time in a very long while, he felt like he might cry. He replaced the phone on the rolling table and located the remote. Pressing the *ON* button, he sought some distraction from the TV. He flipped through the channels, then the loud jangling of the telephone almost startled him.

He lifted the receiver, hoping it wasn't Mackenzie Sabino. That's about all he needed right now.

"Yeah, hello?"

"Wink, it's me. Hey, look, I'm, well, I'm sorry about what I said. I hit an all-time low rubbing your injuries in your face like that."

Hearing Brent's apology, Kevin swallowed hard. What was wrong with him anyway? When had he become such a softie? "Forget it."

"Okay, it's forgotten. Get better, you hear?"

"Will do."

Hanging up the phone for the second time, Kevin couldn't restrain the tears that blurred his vision. He squeezed his eyes shut. Then, the oddest feeling overtook him. He suddenly yearned for Lara, wishing she were at his bedside, "fawning all over him." She made him think everything was going to be okay. Her presence comforted him.

My head must be a mess. I've turned into a regular sissy.

Clearing his thoughts, Kevin willed himself to fall asleep.

ﻪﺀ

"Okay, I admit it. I never got over my childhood crush on Kevin Wincouser—and I probably never will. He was the first and only guy who treated me with dignity and respect when I was a chubby, self-conscious junior-higher." Hiking the strap of Tim's video-camera case back onto her shoulder, she glanced at Polly who walked beside her. "There. Are you happy?"

"After ten hours of listening to your denial. . .yeah, I'm happy now."

Smiling, Lara rolled her eyes as they neared the trailer in which Brent lived. Another cowboy on the grounds had pointed it out to them.

They reached the door, and Polly knocked just as Lara's cell phone rang. Fishing it from her purse, she pushed the tiny green button, answering the call.

"Hi, it's Tim. I'm at the hospital. . ."

Sheer dread poured over Lara. "Is Kevin all right?"

"He's fine. But he wants to talk to you. I'll put him on."

At the pause, Lara waved to Brent who had answered the door and was now beckoning them inside.

"I'll be right there," she said, and a moment later, she heard Kevin's voice.

"So you're in South Dakota."

Lara grinned. "That's right."

"What made you go?"

Since her friend had stepped into the large trailer, Lara decided to divulge the truth. "Do you remember meeting my friend Polly?"

"Umm. . ."

"She stopped in while I was visiting you last week, and I introduced her."

"I'm sorry, Lara, I don't recall."

She heard the drowsiness in his voice. "That's all right.

You were pretty out of it the evening she showed up. But anyway, this trip was Polly's idea. She's rather, um, attracted to Brent, and that's putting it mildly."

"How does she know Brent?"

"She doesn't. I mean, she's seen him get thrown from a bull, and she's talked to him twice." Lara started giggling, realizing how silly it must seem to Kevin. "Sounds like true love, eh?"

"You're kidding me. Your friend? I thought maybe it was you."

"Me? No!"

Before Lara could even wonder about the remark, Brent appeared at the trailer's door. "You comin' in?"

Lara met his gaze and nodded. "I'm talking to Kevin. I'll be right there."

"Lara, listen to me. I want you to be careful, okay? I have a feeling Brent wants to settle an old score, and I'd hate to see you get hurt. He and I had a conversation this morning, and well, I've been thinking about things all day."

"That's really nice of you to be concerned, Kev, but. . ." Lara watched Brent descend the three metal stairs that led down from the trailer before he strode in her direction. ". . .I'll be fine."

"Keep your guard up."

"I always do."

An instant later, Brent reached out and snatched Lara's cell phone.

"What do you think you're doing?" Surprise and indignation caused her to gape at the man.

"Wink? It's me. I don't mean to be rude, but this little social worker is off duty right now. Call back later, after the rodeo tonight, and I'll catch you up on the current standings." Without waiting for a reply, he dropped her phone into her purse. Then, taking hold of Lara's elbow, he guided her toward the trailer. "Wink'll survive for a couple of days. You need a break, a chance to have some fun and enjoy yourself."

Lara bristled. She didn't appreciate being bossed as though she were a little girl. Pulling out of his grasp, she stepped up into the trailer. She'd never been inside what was commonly known as a "fifth wheel," and the sight impressed her, even though it smelled sort of weird—like strong coffee, leather boots, and horseflesh intermingled with dirty socks.

Out of politeness, Lara tried not to grimace as she glanced around. The trailer was much bigger inside than she imagined. To the right was a cozy living room where Polly stood chatting with Quincy. On her immediate left was a small kitchenette and a narrow hallway led away from it to the back of the trailer where Lara assumed the bedrooms were located.

"Welcome to our humble abode," Quincy said with a grin. He extended his right hand, and Lara took it. "Didn't think I'd see you again so soon, but I'm glad for it. Have a seat."

"Thanks."

"Here, let me take your bags," Brent said.

"No, thank you." Lara lowered herself into one of the two swivel rockers and placed the leather-encased video camera and her purse right beside the chair.

"Oh, now, don't be sore at me because I ended your phone call," Brent said, sporting a charming grin. "Wink can be a demanding guy, and Polly just got done telling Quincy and me that you two wanted a little excitement this weekend."

"Can't get more exciting than the bull-riding competition," Quincy added with a laugh. "Would you two ladies like something to drink? A can of pop?"

"No, thanks," Polly replied.

Lara declined the offer as well. She could feel Brent's penetrating stare, but she refused to validate his boorish behavior with even a brief glance. It troubled her that Kevin had taken the time to warn her about the "score" Brent wished to settle, and a heartbeat later, Lara wanted nothing more than to turn tail and go home. This was a stupid idea. Why had she let Polly talk her into it?

"Looks like a camera in that black leather case. Is it?"

Lara drew herself from her thoughts and nodded in reply to Quincy's question. "I volunteer at a ranch for physically challenged kids. When the weather isn't good for riding, we'll play games or watch a movie. The original version of *National Velvet* is one of my kids' favorites. They love any story involving horses, so I thought I'd film the rodeo tonight. The kids will enjoy seeing it."

"That's mighty thoughtful of you," Quincy said. "If you'd like, Quincy the Clown can do a little juggling for the kids."

"Anything to get on camera," Brent quipped.

Lara ignored him. "A juggling act would be great. Thanks." She looked over at Polly whose gaze seemed glued on a certain handsome bull rider. A feeling of disquiet plumed inside of her, and Lara stood. "Well, I guess we should be on our way."

"What?" Polly gave her an incredulous glare.

"I'm hungry," Lara told her with a meaningful glare. "And these gentleman need to get ready for their performances tonight."

"Honey, that's five hours away," Brent said. "We've got plenty of time. But if you'd like something to eat, there's a place nearby that serves up some of the best barbeque beef you've ever tasted."

"Mmm, that sounds good," Polly replied, standing to her feet.

Lara felt the invisible noose around her neck tightening.

"Quincy, want to come along?" Brent asked.

"No, I think I'll let you tend to our guests while I take a quick nap."

"All right, then." Brent gave Lara and Polly an engaging grin. "Let's go."

ten

"I don't like him. He acts like an egomaniac."

Sitting at the picnic table across from Lara, Polly gave her a disappointed pout. "Brent took our orders and went up to buy the food. He's paying. I think he's a gentleman."

Lara glanced over her friend's left shoulder and saw Brent waiting his turn in line at the service window. Located on the far side of the vast ranch on which the rodeo took place, Dakota Dave's BBQ was only a little bigger than a hut in a row of food stops and lemonade and beer stands.

"I still don't like him."

"What happened to 'love your neighbor as yourself' and 'forgiving one another as God, for Christ's sake, forgave us'?"

"All right, all right. You don't have to Scripture-whip me."

"Well?"

Lara shrugged. "I just don't appreciate Brent's macho demeanor. He acts like he's used to women falling at his feet because he's a big rodeo star, and he's wondering why we're not swooning."

"Hey, speak for yourself."

Lara rolled her eyes at the tart reply.

"Okay, fine. You don't like one particular quality about Brent. But you can still be nice and a good Christian witness to him."

"I just feel like going back home."

"Why?"

Picking at the splintery top of the table, Lara shrugged.

"You're going to let a macho cowboy steal your joy? That's

75

silly, Lara. Let's just enjoy ourselves."

Lara glanced across the table and noticed Polly's short, walnut-colored brown hair shimmering in the afternoon sunshine. She was right. No one could steal Lara's joy unless she allowed him to—and she wouldn't.

"We're in South Dakota at a rodeo. How cool is that!" Polly declared. "Wait until I tell everyone on Monday what I did over the weekend."

Lara grinned. "Yeah, we're finally doing something out of the ordinary." She glanced over her friend's shoulder and saw their host heading toward their table. "Here comes Brent."

Polly sat back, straightened her shirt, combed her fingers through her hair, and Lara laughed.

"You're a hoot."

Polly replied with an impish wink.

"Here we are, Ladies," Brent said, setting down a cardboard tray. "If this isn't the best barbeque you've ever tasted, I'll eat your sandwich for you."

Another laugh escaped Lara, and she felt herself begin to relax. Brent set a plastic cup of lemonade in front of her and handed her a straw before offering her a foil wrapped sandwich.

"Thanks."

"You bet." Brent served Polly in the same manner.

"Thank you."

"You're very welcome."

"Should I ask the blessing, or would you like to do the honors, Brent?"

He paused. "Um, you go ahead."

Polly bowed her head, and Lara followed suit. "Thank you, Lord God, for this meal. Thank you for Brent who purchased it for us. We ask that You protect him tonight as he competes in the bull-riding championship. Bless him. . .and Lara and me. In Jesus' name, amen."

"Amen," Lara echoed.

She looked up just in time to see Brent lift his gaze. As they began eating, Lara sensed his discomfort.

"Are you a Christian?" Before she could stop it, the question bubbled out of her mouth. "I, um, hope I'm not being too personal."

"I went to church as a kid," Brent said, taking a large bite of sandwich.

"This barbeque is delicious," Polly said.

Lara's mouth was full, so she nodded.

"You ladies like it?"

"Very much."

"Mmm-hmm. . ."

Brent chuckled. "You even sound like you're enjoying it, Lara."

She swallowed, smiled, and stuck the straw into her plastic glass of lemonade. "Now, getting back to my question. . ."

"About religion?" Brent asked with a glance in her direction, "Wink told me you're a born-again Christian, so I imagine you're looking for recruits."

"All the time."

Polly laughed. "We try not to be obnoxious about it. I'm a born-again Christian too."

"I figured," Brent replied. "It's like that old 'birds of a feather' cliché."

"So, are you or aren't you?" Lara felt rather sassy. It must have been the ten hours she'd spent in the car with Polly.

Pushing up on the rim of his black Stetson, Brent peered at Lara. The expression on his face said he was contemplating her inquiry. "I guess I'm a Christian like some people are Irish. It's in my background, but I don't think about it too much."

"You seem to be confusing religious beliefs with heritage,"

Lara pointed out. "Being Irish isn't something you can control. Becoming a Christian involves exercising your will."

His brown eyes locked on Lara, Brent narrowed his gaze.

Polly touched his forearm. "If you'd prefer not to discuss this issue, we can talk about something else."

"No, that's okay. I don't shy away from controversial topics." He smiled at Polly, then looked back at Lara. "Okay, Little Social Worker, why don't you tell me all about being a Christian, and I'll tell you whether I am one or not."

The challenge caused Lara to smile with delight. God had just flung open a door of opportunity that she couldn't—or wouldn't—pass up. After a glance at Polly, and seeing the prayerful expression on her friend's face, Lara opened her purse and extracted a gospel tract.

"This is pretty simplistic," she stated apologetically. "I use this pamphlet to talk to my kids about Jesus."

"The kids on the ranch?"

Lara nodded. "God's plan of salvation is so easy that children can even comprehend it. Look—" She directed his attention to the tract. "There are four things you've got to understand in order to become a Christian. One, you're a sinner. We're all sinners. No one's perfect, right?"

Brent nodded. "Right."

"Two, sin has to be punished. When you were a kid did you get spankings when you were naughty?"

"Sure did."

"Same thing, except sin is punishable by eternal death in an awful place called Hell." When Brent didn't reply, Lara continued. "Three, Jesus took the punishment for our sin when He died on the cross. I tell my kids that Jesus took the spanking we were supposed to get from our Heavenly Father so we didn't have to get punished."

Brent pursed his lips, thinking it over.

"Four, anyone can be saved if he or she will just ask."

"That's it?" Brent gave her a suspicious look.

"Yep." Lara pushed the small, colorful pamphlet towards him. "You can keep this tract. There are some Bible verses on the back that you can look up and read whenever you get a chance."

"Brent," Polly began, "was there ever a time in your life that you asked Jesus Christ to save you?"

"No, not that I can recall."

"Well, will you give it some thought?"

He nodded, then balled up the foil from his sandwich. "But if what you're saying is true, and those four things are what it takes to be a Christian, then how come no one's told me till now?"

"Maybe your heart wasn't ready to receive the Good News until now," Polly replied.

"Hmm." A grin tugged at the corners of Brent's mouth. "You know what? Instead of hospital work, maybe you two should have gone into sales."

☙

Kevin lay awake, holding the telephone to his ear. After five rings, Brent finally answered.

"About time you picked up."

"Wink?"

"Yeah, it's me. Where've you been? It's one o'clock in the morning."

"I've been out having a good ol' time. Just walked in, as a matter of fact."

In his mind's eye, Kevin could see the trailer he shared with Brent, Quincy, and Jimmy.

Jimmy! He remembered him.

"My memory's comin' back."

"That's a good thing."

"So what kind of 'good ol' time' were you out having?"

"Well, I'm now in second place, Wink. That was cause for celebration, don't you think?"

"Yeah. Congratulations." Kevin tried to raise his right hand, but the limb felt like it had been filled with cement. He was beginning to fear he'd never ride again.

I'll ride again. Of course I'll ride again! Sheer determination gripped his heart. He'd rather die than give up rodeoing.

"Lara and Polly are real nice girls," Brent was saying.

Hearing Lara's name, Kevin forced himself to pay attention.

"They're the kind of women a guy wouldn't mind taking home to meet his mother."

"If he *had* a mother." Kevin's mom was dead, and Brent's left home when he was a boy, never to be heard from again. Neither of them were "Mama's boys."

"You know what I'm getting at."

"I think I do. You'd better have Quincy tell you a bedtime story about one of his three disastrous marriages again."

"Oh, right." Brent chuckled. "I've heard enough of them stories to last me a good part of forever. And speaking of. . ."

"Forever?" Kevin frowned, wondering where all this was going.

"Yeah, Lara and Polly tried to sell me on their faith. Did a pretty good job too. I promised to take 'em to the sunrise church service tomorrow morning. I can't believe I actually said I'd crawl out of bed at the crack of dawn on a Sunday morning."

"It'll be tough, especially if you've been drinking."

"Wink, are you kidding? I haven't had a drop of alcohol. I've been in the company of two Christian women all night. Well, and one mean, angry bull."

Kevin chuckled, and the left side of his head felt sort of weird. It didn't hurt, exactly.

"You know, I was thinking. I'll be thirty years old in less

than six months. Maybe it's time to settle down."

Kevin could hardly believe what he'd just heard. Was his mind playing tricks on him? Was he hallucinating?

Was Brent hallucinating?

"I'm of the persuasion you *have* been drinking, my friend—or indulging in something else."

"Nothing, Wink. I've never been more sober in my life. What about you? You ever give marriage a thought?"

"Maybe just a thought, then my sanity returned."

"What about Christianity? Ever think about it?"

"Sure. My parents were Christians, so was my brother—"

"How come you never told me you had a brother?"

"'Cause we kind of disowned each other."

"Well, better not tell Little Miss Social Worker that, or she's liable to initiate some sort of kiss-and-make-up session." Brent laughed.

Kevin, on the other hand, didn't find the remark a bit amusing. His eyelids suddenly grew heavy. The shot the nurse had given him a half-hour ago was beginning to affect him. "Lara already knows about my brother and me. She grew up with me and Clayt. Remember?" He paused, thinking over Brent's "Little Miss Social Worker" comments. "Sounds like you and Lara aren't getting along so well." In some odd way, the notion comforted Kevin.

"What makes you say that? We're getting along just fine."

Disappointment engulfed him. Lara wasn't Brent's type. His friend had to realize that much.

"It's just too bad she's had a crush on you since her junior-high years."

Kevin frowned. "What? Why is it too bad?"

"'Cause she's still got a crush on you, that's why. But isn't that the way it always goes? If I'm even remotely interested in a woman, it turns out she's got eyes for you."

"You're interested in Lara?"

"I'm not telling you anything about anyone I might be interested in," Brent growled, and Kevin imagined him clenching his jaw while his brown eyes sparked with contained fury. "After what you did with Emily, you're lucky I'm even speaking to you."

"I didn't do anything with Emily—except kiss her after she flung herself at me."

"You're a liar."

"No, Friend, *she's* the liar."

A long pause filled the airspace. "Well, look, it doesn't matter anymore. Neither does Emily. But I will say this—the man who lassoes Lara Donahue's heart won't have to worry about her being unfaithful."

"No, I don't suppose he will." Kevin felt like he'd been socked in the gut.

"And I can contend with a schoolgirl crush. It's nothing compared to true love, right?"

"Leave her alone, Brent. Don't try to get back at me by using Lara."

Brent chuckled. "Is that what you think? Listen, Pal, I have a lot more integrity than you give me credit for." Another pause. "I'm not like you."

Moments later, the phone line went dead, and Kevin felt a deep regret fill his soul. Memory after memory rushed forth like waves against a shoreline. He'd been and done all the things he learned as a kid that God condemned, and yet Brent had been a true friend through it all.

Until the situation with Emily occurred—but that hadn't been Kevin's fault.

Still, in spite of his self-defense, sadness washed over him. The word "integrity" described nothing about Kevin Wincouser. He was about as honorable as a rattlesnake.

Oh, God, why did You let me live? The world would be a lot better off without me in it.

On that dark thought, he tumbled off into a restless sleep.

eleven

After the uplifting sunrise service, Polly convinced Brent to eat breakfast with them instead of returning to his bed as he'd threatened to do ever since they took their seats in the grandstands. However, after consuming several cups of coffee at a quaint diner in town, he came to life. Still, as they drove back to the Cyprus Ranch on which the rodeo was held, Lara had to wonder if anything from this morning's message penetrated his heart. The gospel couldn't have been presented any clearer, and Lara rejoiced that Brent had not only heard God's plan of salvation from her and Polly, but from another cowboy too—a cowboy-preacher. But had Brent been too tired to comprehend the truth?

"Why are you frowning so hard, Lara?"

He's watching me. . .again. Embarrassed, she looked up from where she sat in the backseat of Brent's black pickup truck and smiled. "Oh, it was nothing. I didn't mean to frown."

Stopping at an intersection, he twisted around and tossed a glance at her, and Lara felt that familiar angst settle around her. Ever since yesterday afternoon, she'd done her best to hang back and try to be invisible, but Brent sought her out time after time. It seemed he paid more attention to her than to Polly—and that wasn't supposed to happen. Worse, Lara had gone from disliking Brent to finding his charm and good looks rather appealing. But each time the thought formed in her head, Kevin's warning rang in her ears. *Brent wants to settle an old score, and I'd hate to see you get hurt.*

Lara recalled that first day up in Kevin's hospital room when

Mackenzie Sabino mentioned that "Wink" had stolen Brent's "girl." But Lara couldn't figure out how Brent would use *her* to settle any score. It wasn't as if Lara was Kevin's present girlfriend, although she imagined she wouldn't mind the title.

Then again, in all reality, maybe she would. Ten years changed people—the years had changed her—and now Lara knew Kevin about as little as Polly knew Brent.

Brent pulled onto the vast ranch, and the truck bumped along dirt roads until it slowed as he steered toward the small colony of trailers and tents. Finally, he parked beside the one in which he lived, pulling in alongside Polly's car.

"You ladies want to come inside for more coffee? Quincy and Jimmy are probably awake by now."

"Actually, I'd like to get some pictures of the horses to take back to my kids," Lara said. Turning to Polly, she added, "Let's go for a quick walk before we go back to the hotel."

Polly bobbed her head. "Okay."

"While you two do that, I'll pack up some of Wink's things," Brent said. "I imagine he'll need 'em once he gets better."

Lara met his deep brown gaze.

"You don't mind taking them to the hospital, do you?"

She blinked, feeling oddly flustered. "No, of course I don't mind."

Lara watched as a slow grin spread across his face before he pivoted and strode toward the trailer. "Don't get lost now."

With a flickering skyward glance, Lara turned to Polly. "How could we possibly get lost?"

"I don't know, but if there's a way, we'll be the ones to do it."

Lara laughed as they took off toward the arena. She hoped Polly hadn't noticed her sudden peculiar behavior with Brent.

Lord, please intervene here. I'm acting like an insipid junior higher with an unattainable schoolgirl crush, and I don't want to hurt Polly for the world. She mulled over her petition, examining her heart. *Lord, is that all I'm capable of—schoolgirl crushes? Will I ever know what it's really like to fall in love?*

"Hey, look. Horses."

Lara gave herself a metal shake and gazed up ahead where she saw a cowboy walking toward them leading two frisky mares. When he got within earshot, Polly asked for his picture with the horses, and the husky man of average height obliged them.

They strolled on, pausing here and there to snap a photograph. Reaching the arena, Lara and Polly stepped inside, and to Lara's delight, some cowboys were perfecting their roping techniques. With her video recorder in hand, she filmed their practice.

"My kids'll love watching this video," Lara said as she and Polly traipsed back to Brent's trailer. More than an hour had lapsed, and the noonday sun rose high in an overcast sky.

"I suppose we should start driving back home soon," Polly murmured, pushing strands of hair off her forehead.

Lara agreed with a nod.

"I had fun this weekend."

"I did too."

Polly glanced Lara's way and grinned. "Then it was a worthwhile trip, wouldn't you say?"

"Uh-huh."

"And just wait until the singles' group hears about our adventure."

Lara laughed. "They'll all wonder why we didn't ask them to come along."

"Oh, yeah, right. Could you imagine *that* field trip?"

Again, Lara had to chuckle. With so many stoic souls in their Christian singles' group, it was amazing anybody had fun. But they did try. Lara had to give them a little credit.

They reached the trailer just as Quincy and Jimmy were exiting.

"Brent's getting worried about you ladies," the younger man said with a boyish grin. "But he should be used to having women run out on him by now."

Quincy gave the youthful cowboy a shove, and Jimmy hooted.

"Don't mind him," Quincy said on a note of apology. He drew in a deep breath. "So, you two are going to be heading home soon, eh? Drive safely now."

"We will," Polly said.

"It was real nice seeing you both again. And, Lara. . ." He turned to face her. "You take care of Wink for us."

"Sure." She smiled. "I'll tell him you all say hello."

"You do that." Quincy gave the rim of his wide brimmed hat a polite tug, then turned on his heel and followed Jimmy.

Lara moved toward Polly's car, preparing to deposit her video camera into the backseat just as Brent emerged from the trailer carrying a large blue suitcase.

"Thought I heard you girls out here," he said with a smile. "Finally found your way back, huh?"

"We were never lost, contrary to popular belief." Polly opened the trunk for him, and Brent set the luggage inside.

Brent chuckled. "That's a good thing." He glanced at Lara. "These are most of Wink's clothes. I packed his socks, underwear, shoes, razor. . .everything he'll need once he's out of the hospital and on his way to meet us wherever we might happen to be at that time. There are also some get-well cards in here from friends and *admirers*."

"Do you travel a lot, Brent?" Polly wanted to know.

"Honey, traveling is my life."

Oh, good, he called her 'Honey.' Lara grinned as she gave the back door of Polly's sedan a push. For the better part of the last twenty-four hours, Lara had been "Honey," and the title felt a little demeaning somehow.

"That's the biggest part of the rodeo. Getting there."

"Do you think you'll be back to see Kevin?" Lara asked.

Folding his arms, Brent leaned up against the car. "Guess it all depends."

"On what?" Polly ventured.

"On whether I'm still speaking to him. You see, me and Wink had a bit of a falling out before his accident." Brent held up a hand, forestalling further questions. "I don't care to discuss the particulars, all right? But I wish Wink a speedy recovery."

"I didn't mean to pry," Polly told him. "I just feel like you're a friend now, so I thought I'd ask."

"I am a friend, and don't you forget it," Brent replied, and Lara didn't miss the warmth of sincerity that entered his brown eyes. She felt glad that he'd bestowed the expression on Polly. "And I hope you girls'll come to another rodeo soon. You've got my itinerary. Illinois isn't so far from Wisconsin."

"A lot closer than South Dakota," Lara quipped.

Brent grinned. "Yep. So maybe you can make that competition. It's over the Fourth of July weekend."

"We'll certainly try," Polly promised, and Lara knew she meant every word.

Brent stepped forward and wrapped Polly in a better than "friendly" embrace. Watching on, Lara wanted to giggle, imagining she'd hear all about the weak knees and pounding heart on the way back to Milwaukee. Moments later, Lara got a hug too.

"Drive careful, now," Brent told them after both women climbed into the car.

"We will," Polly promised.

Lara couldn't stop smiling as they drove off the Cyprus Ranch. *Thank You, God, for turning things around.*

❧

The next day, Monday, proved a veritable challenge for Lara. She felt tired from the long hours of traveling over the weekend, and the number of patients who required her services caused her to forego a lunch break and work a couple hours of overtime.

When she finally punched out, she decided to go straight home and skip a visit with Kevin. She figured if she missed one night it wouldn't matter. Maybe he'd even feel relieved if she didn't go up to the floor and see him tonight. But as she walked toward the parking structure, she felt a tweak in her spirit, as if she was disregarding a certain, important responsibility. Of course, that was silly. Kevin wasn't her responsibility.

But he was her friend.

Expelling an audible sigh, Lara pivoted and strode in the opposite direction. After walking through several meandering hallways, she reached the hospital elevators. However, when she arrived on Kevin's floor, she discovered he'd been transferred to the Rehab Unit, so she made her way over there. Finding Kevin's new room, she entered to find him sitting in a wheel chair. Except for his glassy stare, he made an encouraging sight. The huge white bandage that had covered his head like a winter cap had been replaced with gauze that now resembled a bandanna.

"You graduated to Rehab. That's great." Lara sat down in the hard-backed chair next to him. "Did you have a good day?"

"Oh, yeah, real good. The highlight was getting my hair washed and brushing my teeth. That's about all the excitement I could handle, though."

Lara laughed and set down her purse and the canvas bag she habitually took to work. She noticed Kevin didn't appear amused. He seemed almost depressed.

"What's wrong, Kev?"

"*What's wrong?*" His blue-eyed gaze pinned her in place. "How can you ask me that, Lara? Look at me. I just turned twenty-nine years old, and I can barely hold my toothbrush."

"You're recovering from a head injury. What do you expect?

It's going to take time for you to get your strength and coordination back. Give yourself a break."

Lara regretted her harsh tone when she saw Kevin's eyes grow misty.

"I'm sorry," she said, resting her hand on his forearm. "I didn't mean to bark at you just now."

Kevin blinked, and a slight grin tugged at the corners of his mouth. "And I don't mean to be such a little sissy."

The phone began to ring before Lara could reply. Kevin looked at it, then at her.

"Want me to answer it, Kev?"

He nodded.

Leaning forward as she stood, Lara kissed his cheek. "You're not a sissy, either." With that, she walked to the metallic beside table and lifted the receiver. "Hello?"

"Hello, yes," the soft feminine voice replied, "I'm looking for Kevin Wincouser."

"Sure, he's right here. Who's calling?"

A pause. "None of your business, who's calling. Put him on."

Lara was taken aback. If she'd "barked" before, this woman was snarling.

"Who is it?" Kevin wanted to know.

Lara covered the mouthpiece of the receiver. She had a good idea as to the caller's identity. "I think it's that red-haired woman."

"Mac?" Kevin made an effort to wag his head. "She's the last person on earth I want to talk to right now. She's been calling here all day."

Lara said nothing.

"Hang up on her."

"Kevin, I can't do that. Our Heavenly Father wouldn't be very pleased with me if I did."

He stared at her with those big Baby Blues, and Lara

suddenly felt thirteen years old again

"Why do you have to be so sweet and nice?" Kevin muttered.

Lara gave him a helpless shrug. She didn't think of herself as "so sweet and nice."

Kevin blew out a long sigh. "Okay, would you mind wheeling me to the phone so *I* can hang up on her?"

Setting down the receiver, Lara tried not to laugh. She walked over to Kevin, and coming to stand behind his wheelchair, she pushed him to the bedside table.

Kevin reached forward with this left arm and grabbed the phone. He lifted it to his ear. "Mac? Don't call here anymore. I don't know when I'll get back in the saddle again, all right? So quit asking!" Without waiting for a reply, he unceremoniously hung up the phone.

"Well, I guess you told her."

"Yeah, for the third time. I doubt she'll listen." He looked up at Lara. "Think you could help me into bed? I'm whipped."

"Sure."

Moving to his left side, Lara helped him stand. Kevin leaned on her to take a heavy step forward. Reaching the bed, he sat down, and Lara straightened the blue printed gown he wore over baggy blue pajama bottoms. She then lifted his right leg up onto the bed while Kevin swiveled on his backside. With the goal painstakingly accomplished, he lay back against his pillows, looking exhausted.

"All that just to get into bed."

"It'll get better day by day."

"And what if it doesn't?" Kevin snapped.

"It will."

Lara lowered herself onto the edge of his sheet-covered mattress. She didn't let his abrasive tone affect her. She'd learned that people handled their illnesses and injuries in all different ways. Some turned weepy, some moaned and complained, and some patients became grumpy ol' bears.

Lara gave Kevin a smile. "Just look at the progress you've made over the last ten days."

He gazed at her through sleepy eyes, and finally, a smile escaped. "As I recall, you were always cheerful. I think that's why I liked having you around when we were kids."

"You did?" Lara felt her face warm with the compliment. "I thought I was just the neighborhood pest, and you were just a nice guy."

"Just a nice guy? Brent said you still have a crush on me. Is that right?"

By now, her cheeks were aflame with embarrassment. "All you cowboys have egos the size of Montana." Lara stood, and Kevin caught her wrist.

"Come on now, Miss Happy-go-lucky. Let's hear the truth."

"Kevin, I haven't seen you in ten years." Lara hoped she was covering her emotions. "How could I possibly still have a crush on you?"

He released his hold and allowed his hand to fall onto the bed's mattress. His expression lost all signs of humor. "Yeah, you got a point there. And I'm not much to look at these days. I might never be. I could end up an invalid for life."

Lara's heart ached for him. "Where's your faith?" She all but whispered the question. "It's times like this that we need the Lord. We draw our strength and determination from Him."

He rolled his head toward the windows, his face turned away from her. "My faith died with my parents, Lara."

She sat back down, realizing the social worker in her wouldn't let her leave him in this frame of mind. "Will you tell me about it—about how you felt after your mom and dad's tragic accident?"

"What's to tell?" He looked at her once more. "Their deaths shook me up, and I couldn't understand why a good God would let two of the most important people in my life die in a catastrophic train wreck. They'd been on their second honeymoon!"

"I know." Lara glanced down at Kevin's calloused hand. She took a few moments to ponder her reply. "Dying is what really stinks about this sin-cursed earth. We're all going to die sometime, and some of us will face painful deaths while others will leave this world peacefully. God said it would happen. So I've concluded it's what we do while we're alive that counts. Remember what Jesus said about things that are 'bound' on earth will be bound in heaven and those things that are 'loosed' on earth will be loosed in heaven?" Lara tipped her head, wondering if Kevin was paying attention. He had his eyes closed. Perhaps he'd decided to ignore her.

But just when she thought the latter was the case, he looked at her as if waiting for her to continue.

"I heard a pastor say the keys that Jesus talks about giving His believers to bind or loose things on earth and in heaven represent opportunities to bring people to Him. So that's our purpose in this life—to lead lost souls to the One who can save them." Lara smiled. "That's *my* purpose, anyway. And if God has to take my life in order for someone else to receive salvation, then I'm willing. It's a cause worth dying for."

Kevin moaned and brought his left hand up, covering his eyes. Then he turned away again.

"Did I upset you? I'm sorry. I didn't mean to."

No reply.

Lara suddenly felt terrible. Even though her tone had been soft, she realized her words may have come across as supercilious and uncaring.

"Kevin?"

He sniffed, sounding suddenly congested.

"Are you all right? Should I call for your nurse?"

His actions were unhurried as he inhaled noisily through

his nose, then wiped his eyes. Lara realized to her horror that Kevin was…*crying*.

She leaned forward, taking his hand in both of hers. "Kev, I'm so sorry. I didn't mean to hurt your feelings."

"Well, you did," he eked out. "But the truth sometimes hurts, doesn't it?"

Lara frowned. "The truth? What do you mean?"

He met her gaze, his eyes red-rimmed and sorrowful. "My parents' thinking matched yours, Lara. They would have given up their lives if it meant even one person got saved."

"Maybe one person *did* get saved. Only God knows."

Kevin lay silent in obvious contemplation. Finally, his eyes moved to Lara's face. He seemed to search her features. Then, at last, he grinned. "You're a special woman, Lara Donahue."

"You're special too." She watched a mischievous twinkle enter his gaze.

"You sure you still don't have a crush on me?"

"Oh, you!" Lara laughed and stood. "That does it. I'm going to visit my friend, Polly, and get some junk food from the vending machines. If you're *lucky*, I'll stop and say good-night on my way out."

Kevin's chuckles followed her out the door. "Hurry back."

twelve

Kevin couldn't say for sure what happened to him the night Lara visited, but for the remainder of the week, he felt less depressed and more determined than ever to get well. Rob, his physical therapist, taught him some strengthening exercises, and Kevin practiced them several times a day. His right arm and leg were showing signs of improvement; however, his speech was still slurred, and frequently, Kevin felt like his mouth couldn't keep up with his mind.

"When do you think I'll get out of this place, Doctor Kitrell?"

The neurosurgery resident looked up from Kevin's chart. "Oh, I'd say a couple of weeks. But I have to be honest with you, it'll be a long time, if ever, before you can compete in a rodeo again."

"What?" Kevin slid himself into a sitting position on his hospital bed. "What are you saying?"

"You suffered a traumatic brain injury, although a fairly mild one, but a bruise to your brain none the less. A bruise forms when blood vessels rupture. As you know, there was blood accumulating around the side of your brain, so we had to insert a drainage tube."

"Yeah, yeah, you don't have to remind me."

It made Kevin a little queasy to think of someone drilling a hole in his skull and sticking a tiny strawlike tube inside. He was just glad the awful thing had been removed a couple of days ago.

"Your last CT scan shows things are healing nicely," Kitrell continued, "but any jolt or bump to your head could cause a reinjury that might have worse effects than those you've already suffered."

"Like?"

"Like seizures, a stroke, permanent paralysis."

"Look, I've had bruises before," Kevin countered. "Plenty of bruises. They heal up and disappear, and you never know they were there. Why's this bruise so different?"

"Think of it like this," Dr. Kitrell said in a curt, no-nonsense tone. "Some athletes tear ligaments in their ankles and knees, and they're unable to return to sports. The same is true with you, except your 'tear' was inside your head."

"No!" Kevin couldn't accept it. He *wouldn't*. He loved rodeoing. It was in his blood. Riding barebacks was his life. "I'll ride again. I'm a two-time world champion, going for three. I'm not about to give up everything I've worked toward for the last ten years. This head injury wants to turn me into a sideline spectator, but I refuse to let it."

"Even if it means sacrificing your health, maybe even your life?"

"Yeah," Kevin replied, undaunted. Then he heard Lara's voice whisper through his memory. *It's a cause worth dying for*. She'd been referring to her part in converting unbelievers to Christ. Kevin, however, had his own cause, one that he was willing to die for—becoming the best bareback champion such as the world had never seen.

"Well, I'd urge you to reconsider," Kitrell said. He slapped the chart shut, and holding it in one hand, he let his arm drop to his side. "Have a good weekend."

Kevin almost laughed. How was it possible that he'd have a good weekend holed up in a hospital room?

Glancing toward the windows, he viewed a dark gray sky. He wondered about Brent, Quincy, and Jimmy and found himself resenting the fact he hadn't heard from any of them in a week—ever since Lara and her friend drove to South Dakota. . .

Kevin's mood plummeted. While he'd received flowers and get-well wishes from friends and fans, he still felt very alone. He thought about the Donahues and how nice it was that Lara and her family took time out from their schedules to visit him. He especially enjoyed conversing with Tim, who loved the rodeo almost as much as Kevin did—and of course Lara, his angel of mercy, who showed up just when he needed her the most. He and Lara had shared some meaningful conversations over the past days. Kevin couldn't ever remember bearing his soul with any woman like he had with Lara.

Lara. As Kevin's thoughts strayed to her, he decided Brent had been correct when he said the guy who lassoed her heart wouldn't have to worry about her faithfulness. Lara was about as loyal and dependable as a hound—of course, that's where the similarities ended. Lara Donahue had grown into a lovely woman. She possessed an inner beauty that Kevin hadn't noticed in the women he'd been acquainted with over the years. Even so, Lara had the words "husband" and "children" written on her future, and Kevin didn't want any part of either one of them. Families meant responsibilities, commitment. . .sacrifice. And what did a guy get in return? A busted up heart—if and when God snatched them away. Just like He did with Kevin's parents. . .

Just like He was doing with the rodeo.

No matter how he summed it up, Kevin felt like an all-around loser.

❧

As the Fourth of July holiday approached, Lara felt as though she were being stretched in two directions. Brent phoned, inviting her and Polly to Cheyenne Days in Galena, Illinois, and of course, Polly wanted to go in the worst way. Polly had even convinced five members of their singles' group that the rodeo was a worthwhile event, so those women planned to make the relatively short drive for a long, fun weekend.

However, Lara wasn't so sure she wanted to join them. For the past several days, Kevin seemed down in the dumps, and Lara hated the thought of him spending July 4th alone. Tim and Amanda offered to smuggle a pizza into the hospital, and since Kevin had gotten the "okay" from his doctor occasionally to leave the rehab floor for the outdoor patio, they'd all be able to watch the fireworks later on in the evening.

"Naw, Lara, that's all right. You don't have to do that," Kevin said when she suggested the pizza plan on the afternoon of July third. "You and your family have already spent an inordinate amount of time with me. I'm sure you've got a life."

Lara regarded him as he sat in a wheelchair wearing faded blue jeans and a light blue crewneck T-shirt with a single navy stripe across the chest. For the last three days, he'd gotten dressed, although Kevin wasn't pleased that it took an hour and some help from a nurse to accomplish what had once taken him mere minutes all by himself.

"Kevin, my life is all about helping other people. Here at the hospital, at church, at home, and at the ranch. I don't mind keeping you company on the Fourth of July."

He shook his blond head, and his blue eyes darkened. "Let's get one thing straight from here on in, okay? I don't need your help, and I sure don't want your pity.

Shocked, Lara gaped at him.

"I'm not a little boy, and I don't need a mommy."

"Fine." She bit back a cynical reply and turned on her professional voice since she didn't trust her emotions. She had thought they were becoming friends—good friends. But it appeared she'd been mistaken. "You know how to contact me if you change your mind. I'm more than happy to be of some assistance to you."

After a parting smile, albeit a forced one, Lara pivoted and exited the room.

"Lara, wait. . ."

She paused just outside his doorway, before slowly turning back around to face him. She fought to keep her expression from revealing the heartache she felt.

"Hey, look, I'm sorry. I shouldn't have said what I did."

"Well, that's obviously how you're feeling, so you needed to tell me. But, just for the record, I never intended to thrust my good deeds on you. I never pitied you, and I certainly didn't mean to act like a mother figure. I only thought that if I were the one stuck in the hospital, I'd welcome some company, and I wouldn't want to spend the Fourth of July by myself." She shrugged. "That's all. But it's no big deal."

Spinning on her heel, she headed for her office. She suddenly felt like that awkward thirteen year old who'd just been ridiculed by the popular kid in school. Kevin's rejection opened the old wound. However, by the time she reached the main floor of the hospital, she'd collected herself, at least for the time being.

Making her way back through the emergency department and into her stuffy little office, Lara decided Cheyenne Days didn't seem like such a bad option for this coming weekend after all.

❧

Watching Lara leave his hospital room, Kevin swallowed a curse. He hadn't meant to hurt her feelings, and he could tell that's exactly what he'd done. It was just that his head ached, and he felt so weary of not being able to accomplish all the things he used to do. Simple things. Like walking, talking without slurring his words, writing, feeding himself without getting most of it dribbled down the front of his shirt.

But I'm going to lick this. I'm going to ride again.

Despite a niggling of doubt that continually threatened to pull him into the dark depths of despair, Kevin imagined the grand welcome he'd receive when he returned to the rodeo circuit. He envisioned the crowd, cheering from the grandstand as the announcer exclaimed how Kevin "Wink" Wincouser had overcome a traumatic brain injury and was now a world champion for the third time in his career!

A knock on the door brought Kevin out of his daydream.

"Hi," said the brunette woman with a sunny smile, "I'm Kathy, the financial counselor. I came to speak with you about your bill. May I come in?"

"Sure, but I've got insurance. I talked to somebody else about it."

"Right. I know that. . ." The woman entered, and Kevin detected her air of self-confidence, ". . .but your insurance company has only agreed to pay a percentage of your bill."

She began to rattle off the specifics of his policy, all of which went zinging right over Kevin's head.

"Okay, okay," he said at last, holding up his left hand to forestall further explanation. "Just tell me the bottom line. What are my out-of-pocket costs?"

"Twelve thousand five hundred and fifty-three dollars and eight-four cents. Now, that's just the hospital bill. You can expect to get a bill from the doctors, radiologists, the lab, ER physicians, and—"

"I'm getting out of here. This *hotel* is much too expensive—and the food isn't even that good."

In spite of the sarcasm, Kevin's thoughts whirred. Getting bucked off that bronc had jeopardized not only his career but his life savings and then some!

He struggled to stand, realizing there was no way he'd walk out of the hospital on his own. He was going to need help. A lot of help. And he'd need a place to stay.

Kevin considered phoning Quincy and asking him to come and fetch him. But even if Quincy agreed, Kevin would need assistance with the basics, and none of his three roommates were likely to volunteer for *that* position.

"I could ask the social worker to come up and talk with you," The financial counselor said. "There might be some federal programs or grants that you qualify for."

He winced. "Um, I don't think the social worker is speaking to me right now."

"Oh?"

Kevin noticed the curious expression on the woman's face and waved off his previous remark. "Never mind. But, um. . ." He cringed before asking his next question. "Will you guys take a credit card?"

thirteen

Kevin pondered his dilemma long after the financial counselor left his room. He figured Mac would bail him out if he called her. She'd probably hop the next plane, pay all his medical bills, and nurse him back to health in her Houston penthouse. Of course, Kevin would most likely have to marry her in return.

He considered the idea for all of two seconds before deciding he wasn't that desperate. He'd much rather eat some humble pie and ask Lara to help him out. She was a sweetheart. She'd forgive him.

Once again, Kevin regretted his harsh words. He knew she didn't pity him—but he felt pitiful—and things were only getting worse.

Maneuvering his wheelchair, which was no easy task with his right arm in its weakened state, he made it to the telephone on the side table. He placed the receiver between his ear and shoulder and punched in a "*0*." The hospital operator then transferred him to Lara's extension. No answer. He hung up, waited a while, and called back. This time he heard Lara's recorded message saying she had left for the day and wouldn't be back in the office until Monday, July seventh.

Great. Kevin hung up the telephone. *Now what do I do?*

❧

"Lara, cheer up, will you?"

From the front passenger seat of the minivan that Polly borrowed from her brother, Lara glanced at her friend who sat behind the wheel. "I'm trying. It's just that Kevin's—"

"He's had a head injury," Polly cut in. "He's recuperating. Of course he's going to say things he doesn't mean." Taking her eyes off the freeway, she met Lara's gaze for a brief moment. "Besides, these rodeo cowboys are the kind of guys who abhor being coddled. I mean, they get bucked off bulls and broncos, then climb right back up into the saddle and get bucked off again."

"They sound like masochists to me," Annmarie Watson said from where she sat in the middle back seat. "But then, again, what can be more charming and romantic than a cowboy?"

"Particularly if he resembles Clint Eastwood."

Lara laughed and leaned over to look into the backseat. "You're dating yourself, Ramona."

The fifty-three-year-old widow feigned an incredulous glare. "And you think that just because I don't open my mouth, nobody will suspect I'm middle-aged? Ha! Just look at all this gray!" For emphasis, Ramona pointed to her short hair, the color of which reminded Lara of chocolate cookies and cream.

"Clint's a has-been," Betsy Krause declared. "Think Brad Pitt."

"He's no cowboy." Ramona smiled, looking dreamy. "Think Paul Newman and Robert Redford—now there's a pair of good-looking *cowboys*."

"Have you seen them lately?" Polly asked as she put on the blinker and changed lanes. "They're old-timers."

"Ah, but in my heart, they'll always be Butch Cassidy and the Sundance Kid."

"I couldn't agree more," said Barb Thomas. She was about the same age as Ramona.

"My favorite cowboy was Glen Campbell in *True Grit*," Karla Stevens declared from her place next to Betsy in the third backseat.

"Another old-timer," Polly muttered, but only Lara heard her. She laughed. "Who's your favorite cowboy?"

Polly gave her a wondering glance. "Brent Yiska, of course. Who's yours?"

"Kevin 'Wink' Wincouser."

Polly shot a curious glance at her. "Are you really stuck on him, Lara?"

She turned and stared out the windshield. "I think I've been stuck on Kevin since I was thirteen years old."

≈a

Kevin spent the Fourth of July alone. He told himself that it was just another day and that he didn't care, but he kept thinking about all the past July fourth holidays he'd celebrated and began feeling depressed and lonely. He remembered Lara's offer and wished once more that he hadn't refused it.

As his thoughts progressed, he recalled some of the heavy conversations he and Lara had over the past couple of weeks. They talked about God—rather, Lara talked about God and what He might be trying to accomplish through Kevin's accident. She said Brent had heard the gospel, not only from her and her friend, but from a preacher at a sunrise service. It was to Kevin's shame that Brent hadn't heard it from his best friend. The truth was Kevin hadn't ever discussed Jesus Christ with anybody—not since he'd left Wisconsin after his parents' death. He focused instead on his career and throwing himself into everything and anything that he suspected would further make him a success. Kevin hadn't allowed himself time to examine his heart, his motives. But now with so much time on his hands and Lara, the social worker, counseling him for free, Kevin couldn't do anything *but* ponder his past and fret over his future.

"It sounds as if you're disappointed with God, perhaps even angry with Him, for allowing your parents' death." The memory of Lara's remarks rang in his ears. "But the sad truth is, we're all going to face death one day, and that's not God's fault." She became pensive for several moments. "Do you remember that verse in Second Peter? 'The Lord is not slow in keeping his promise, as some understand slowness. He is patient with you, not wanting anyone to perish, but everyone to come to repentance.'?"

Kevin remembered, although he'd forgotten in which book of the Bible that passage could be found.

"Well, not everyone will come to repentance. That's a fact. There are people who have rejected God's gift of salvation, and they'll suffer for an eternity because of it. They've made a decision that's outside of God's will."

"What are you getting at, Lara?" Kevin had asked, feeling impatient.

"I'm trying to say that bad things happen in this life, and they're not God's fault. There is nothing wicked or bad in God's character. Nothing. Everything about God is good. So stop blaming Him for your parents' death."

Kevin had disputed her claim that he blamed God for *anything* and Lara backed off.

Seated in the vinyl-padded recliner positioned near the window, Kevin had to grin. Lara gave in way too easy. She should have stood her ground, but instead she had changed the subject.

And here I am thinking about it.

Kevin suddenly realized Lara's silence had been more affective than a standoff.

I suppose she's right, Lord. Maybe I have been blaming You for taking away my parents and busting up my family. I never even knew I was holding such a grudge..."

Kevin's eyes grew misty. Twenty-nine years old and he still grieved his parents' death. He also missed his brother Clayt's camaraderie. But in the next moment, the magnitude of his selfishness filled his being. Realization set in.

All these years, he only saw what he lost and not what he took from others. Kevin had looked inward, at himself, at his desires and ambition, not upward—not at the Lord. He had tossed aside the values and teachings his parents, teachers, and youth pastors had given him. They'd invested a part of themselves in him, and he'd never given anything back.

For the last decade, he never looked outward the way Lara and her family did. Kevin couldn't remember the last time he did someone a favor without having to be asked first. When did he last consider someone else's wellbeing before his own?

His heart broke. *Oh, God, forgive me. . .*

ช

The sun had set behind the large tent on the fairgrounds. Inside a band consisting of a fiddle, banjo, and guitar players, along with a percussionist, performed a lively Americana folk tune, part of a grand Fourth of July celebration that lasted all weekend. A parade and fireworks had marked the celebration yesterday, and an arts and crafts exhibition, a tractor pull, and an afternoon rodeo had been on today's agenda. But now, as evening fell, battery-operated lanterns illuminated the evening, and from where Lara sat at a rectangular table surrounded by her friends and cajoling cowboys, she felt like she was on the set for the musical *Seven Brides for Seven Brothers*.

Glancing to her right, Lara caught snippets of Polly's conversation with a guy named Austin. He was a stocky fellow with jet-black hair who was very open about his faith in Christ. Austin's presence put Lara somewhat at ease since Brent was at his flirty best tonight. And being the dashing cowboy he was, Brent took each lady to the dance floor and, one by one, charmed his way into their hearts. Barb and Ramona each declared that Paul Newman couldn't hold a candle to Brent Yiska; however, the two were now engrossed in a jovial conversation with Quincy.

Brent and Annmarie returned from their dance. Since it had been an upbeat tempo, they were both breathing hard when they sat down at the table. Brent claimed the chair to Lara's immediate left—the one Annmarie had occupied minutes before. After a moment's frown of confusion, Annmarie grabbed her purse and sat down on the other side of the table next to Betsy.

Lara knew her turn to dance with Brent was coming, and she stifled a cringe. Up until now, she'd been able to keep her distance. She'd even avoided looking Brent's way because each time she did, he would catch her eye and wink or give her a winsome grin. Lara had to admit it wouldn't be hard to fall under Brent's spell. But each time that thought surfaced, reality tapped Lara on the shoulder. One of her best friends had her heart set on winning his affections, and Lara wouldn't hurt Polly for the world. Besides, Kevin's warning kept echoing in her ears: *I have a feeling Brent wants to settle an old score. . .*

"You having fun?" Brent nudged her with his elbow, jerking Lara from her musings.

"Yeah, I'm having a great time. How about you?"

"Yep." He blew out an audible sigh. "And I'm getting my exercise for the day."

"I'll say." Lara smiled, then glanced at Polly who still chatted with Austin.

"Hey, Jimmy, hand me that pitcher."

The fresh-faced cowboy grinned and pushed the plastic pitcher half-filled with golden liquid toward Brent.

"No, give me the other one, the cola. I drank too much last night, and I don't want to be hungover in the morning when I escort these pretty ladies to church."

Lara thought he'd seemed happier and perhaps friendlier last night, although she hadn't noticed that he was drunk. She almost felt like she'd been duped. Here she'd thought the laughter they all shared at the fireworks was genuine, when in actuality it had been manufactured by alcohol.

"You coming to church again, Brent?" Austin leaned around Polly as he posed the question.

"Yeah, I figured I would."

"That's two Sundays in a row."

Brent didn't reply but filled the plastic cup in his hand with cola.

"Hey, Brent," Jimmy said, sitting forward so his chest nearly rested on the tabletop, "you're not becoming one of those FCC guys, are you?"

"What's FCC?" Polly wanted to know.

"Fellowship of Christian Cowboys," Austin replied. His barrel-like chest swelled in a silent challenge. "And so what if he is? When you're on the back of a one-ton bull, it's not a bad thing to have the Lord with you. Can't argue with that, now can you, Jimmy?"

"Um, no, guess not."

Lara heard Brent chuckle before he chugged down his cola. Then he changed the subject.

"Tell us how Wink's doing, Lara."

"I guess he's okay." She knew with all the federal regulations concerning patient confidentiality that she couldn't give specifics. "You should give him a call."

"Yeah, I've been meaning to." Brent paused, and other conversations around the table resumed. "But what do you mean you 'guess' he's okay? I was under the impression you went to see him everyday."

"I tried, but—" Lara waved a hand in the air. "Oh, don't ask, Brent." She didn't feel like discussing her last conversation with Kevin. It still kind of stung.

"Wink hurt your feelings, huh?"

Lara didn't reply. It smarted even to admit the truth.

The band began playing a slower tune, and when the melodious strains reached her ears, Lara guessed Brent's next thought. Scooting her chair back, she decided to head for the restroom where she could wait out the set. But when she stood, Brent caught her wrist.

"I owe you a dance, Miss Social Worker."

"You don't owe me a thing, and I'm really not a good dancer. In fact, I can't even think of the last time I danced with someone. . ."

Brent ignored her ramblings and led her onto the wooden platform over which the huge tent had been erected. Feeling inept, Lara dreaded what was about to come. She'd danced all of three times in her entire life. She'd never been asked to her high school prom, and she didn't frequent establishments that sported dancing. She wasn't a square dancer, didn't practice ballet, and she wasn't into the aerobic dances at health clubs, although the latter would probably do her some good.

Brent found an opening and stopped. When he turned around and faced her, Lara tried again to explain.

"I really don't know how to dance."

He took her protest in stride. "It's easy. You put your left hand on my shoulder, like so, and I put my arm around your waist. . ."

Lara felt like she was about to break out in a sweat as Brent pulled her closer to him.

"Now, you put your right hand in mine."

Doing as he bid her, Lara shook her head. "I did know *that* much, okay?"

"Okay." Brent wore a hint of a smirk. "Now just move side-to-side. Follow my lead. I promise I won't try anything fancy."

Lara swallowed her objections, not wanting to be rude, but self-consciousness enveloped her like Brent's embrace. However, all her friends were dancing, why did she feel so uncomfortable? Perhaps it was her lack of experience.

Brent held her nearer to him, and Lara felt his hand come to rest in the center of her back. Her chin was level with his shoulder, and suddenly, the sight that caught her gaze made her pause. There, just ten feet away, stood Polly, dancing with Austin.

"What's wrong?" Brent stepped back and frowned.

"Um, oh, nothing. Sorry."

Brent swung her around so he could see what she'd been gaping at, and Lara laughed when she tripped over the toe of his boot.

"Hey, I thought you weren't going to try anything fancy."

Brent chuckled. "My apologies. Were you surprised to see Polly dancing with Austin?"

"Yes." Lara didn't see any point in fibbing. In fact, now seemed a perfect time to divulge the entire truth. "Polly's got a major crush on you."

"She does not!"

"Yes, she does. Haven't you noticed?"

A slight frown creased his dark brow. "Guess not."

"Even Quincy noticed."

"I suppose I'm a little short on smarts where women are concerned."

"Oh, right," Lara teased. "You're just so used to ladies ogling you that you don't even notice anymore."

Jerking her forward, he tickled her, and Lara let out a yelp. Several heads turned, and Lara wanted to die of embarrassment.

"Quit steppin' on her feet, Brent," a nearby cowboy admonished in jest. "You're gonna hurt the poor thang!"

After a quelling look at the other man, Brent peered into Lara's now flaming face. She met his gaze, and they shared a laugh. But all too soon, she read something in his brown eyes that made her feel uneasy.

Looking away, Lara searched for Polly who was still in Austin's arms. Polly happened to catch her eye and smiled and waved. She didn't seem a bit unhappy at the dance partner situation.

"Honestly, Lara, I had no idea Polly was interested in me," Brent said so close to her ear that his warm breath sent shivers down her spine. "I hope I didn't do anything to offend her."

"I don't think you did." Lara hoped she didn't offend her friend, either.

A few moments passed, then Brent lowered his head so his cheek rested against hers. Lara tried not to grimace, but she felt so torn. On one hand, it felt so romantic, dancing with Brent to a lovely melody, that she wanted to enjoy this moment. But on the other, it just didn't seem right.

"Relax, Lara."

"I'm trying."

Brent took half a step backwards and gave her a curious stare. "What's the matter?"

Again, Lara decided on the truth. "Well, in addition to Polly having a crush on you, Kevin told me that you've got a score to settle, and I just don't want to get caught in the crossfire."

"He said that?" Brent's expression darkened. He stopped in midstride. "Let's get one thing straight, Honey. I would never use another person to. . .*settle a score*. That might be Wink's way, but it's not mine."

The spark of indignation in his eyes caused Lara to believe him. "Okay, things are straight."

"Good." He drew Lara close to him once more. "Guess it's good we cleared the air."

"Yeah," she said, watching Polly and Austin. Her thoughts were in a jumble. "Guess it's good. . ."

The dance ended, and Lara stepped backwards just as

another woman approached them. She was red, white, and blue, from her snug denim jeans, red cotton t-shirt, and white cowboy hat. Her long blond hair flowed down past her shoulders in silky waves.

"Brent," she drawled with a pout, "I've been waitin' all night for you to ask me to dance. So, after two Old Fashions, I decided to ask you."

He chuckled, then his gaze slid to Lara in a moment of uncertainty.

"Go ahead and dance if you want to, Brent," Lara said. "I'm sitting this one out anyway."

"You sure?"

"More than sure."

She gave him what she hoped was a gracious smile, but inside, Lara felt troubled—and it would take the next few hours for her to figure out why.

fourteen

Back in their hotel room later that night, Lara managed to corner Polly in the ivory-tiled lavatory while their two room-mates watched TV.

"I've got to talk to you." Lara entered and closed the door behind her.

"I've got to talk to you too!" Dressed in an oversized night-shirt, Polly had removed her makeup and was now smearing cream onto her face.

"What's going on? I mean, you and Austin tonight behaved as though only the two of you existed."

Polly lowered her gaze.

"I told Brent that you were interested in him, and by the time we left the fairgrounds, I'm sure he thought I was either delusional or terribly misinformed."

"You told him?"

"Well, yeah. He had no idea."

Polly swept her gaze upward. "That figures. Well, it doesn't matter anyhow."

"What?" Lara smacked her forehead with her palm.

"I don't know if Austin is the one, but—"

"Polly, I think I'm seeing a pattern here. Remember back about eight months ago when you thought Peter Fitzgerald was *the one*?"

"I know, I know. . ." Polly held up a hand to forestall further reprimand. "It's just that I've been praying so hard. You know how much I want to get married and have kids. I expect God to answer my prayers and send Mr. Right directly into my path."

Lara lowered herself onto the edge of the bathtub. She could relate to her friend. Lara wanted to get married and raise a family too. She had been praying for a husband since she began college. She knew God would answer her prayer in His perfect time, but she, like Polly, was still waiting.

"I don't mean to be capricious," Polly told her as an expression of chagrin shadowed her features.

"You're not. I understand more than you know. My dream is to marry a man who loves the Lord first and me second."

"Maybe it's Brent." An ambiguous smile curved Polly's lips. "I'm not blind, you know. I can tell he's fond of you."

"He doesn't even know me," Lara countered. She couldn't help wondering if Polly's new interest in Austin had something to do with Brent's solicitations. "I have a feeling it's a game to him, a challenge to see if he can sweep the naive Christian social worker off her feet. But deep down I think Brent's really in love with the thrill of an eight-second bull ride." She paused, mulling over her statement, then added, "Unfortunately, I think Kevin is in love with an eight-second ride too."

Polly laughed. "Must you analyze *everything*?"

"Of course." Lara stood and faced her friend, then grinned. "*One* of us has to be practical."

"Oh, I guess that's true," Polly said, feigning a reluctant tone.

Lara grinned and left the bathroom, but she sensed some tension between her and Polly. Entering the bedroom of the suite all seven ladies shared, Lara saw that Barb and Ramona had already fallen asleep in one of the two double beds. Out in the living room area, Annmarie, Betsy, and Karla were chatting before bunking down on the hideaway couch and the rollaway bed they'd requested from the hotel.

Picking up the remote, Lara turned off the TV and crawled into the bed she would share with Polly tonight. A few minutes ticked by, and she listened to the other ladies' soft snoring. Lara yawned, turned over, then prayed about this awkward situation.

Men. What a pack of trouble they caused. But in her heart, Lara believed that what she'd told Polly was true; Brent's attentions had to be part of some sort of charade. Lara wasn't his type—and he definitely wasn't hers. Moreover, the rodeo circuit with its competitive pressure to win, to be the best, and its rowdy lifestyle held no appeal for Lara.

Then there was the traveling. . .

Tonight, she'd heard a cowboy fondly refer to himself as a "rodeo gypsy." Lara imagined driving from city to city, town to town, and concluded it wasn't how she desired to spend her life. Lara wanted stability and a husband who came home to her every night—a husband who didn't drink beer and shots of whiskey, whose eye didn't wander, and one who didn't slow dance with cute little blonds.

No, rodeoing could never be even a fragment of her world.

જ

The next morning, Lara had to admit she felt impressed with Brent in spite of her decision about him and his profession. He'd roused himself in time for tent meeting, otherwise known as Sunday morning church service. He'd even showed up carrying a Bible! Since Lara had strategically situated herself between Betsy and Ramona, Brent took a seat on the end bench beside Polly.

Today's message was about making a difference for Christ and how believers need to behave in a manner that counters worldly trends and standards.

"It might not be popular, and you might lose a few friends," the rugged-looking cowboy-preacher told the small crowd. "But God will honor your obedience. Try it and see."

Thinking back on last night and even the Fourth of July, Lara had to admit she had wanted to *fit in*. She wanted

Kevin's friends to like her—she wanted Kevin to like her. She felt as though she'd been an outcast all her life, but the preacher's next words humbled her.

"Our life's purpose as Christians is to glorify the Savior in everything we do. Praise God we live in the United States of America where we are free to assemble together and worship Jesus Christ. Many a life has been lost over the centuries in order for us to enjoy this freedom."

Cheers broke out along with applause, and some affixed a hearty *amen* to the statement.

When the service ended, Lara and the others ambled out of the tent. The plan was to find a restaurant serving brunch before they checked out of the hotel and headed home.

"Lara!"

Nearing Polly's brother's minivan, she paused while Brent caught up to her.

"Hey, listen, I phoned the hospital right before coming here, and I was told Wink checked out yesterday morning."

"What?" Lara felt sure she hadn't heard him right.

"That's what they told me."

"But he wasn't in any condition to leave the hospital!"

Brent narrowed his brown-eyed gaze. "Where do you suppose Wink would go? I checked with Quincy and Jimmy. None of us got phone calls."

"I don't know." Lara's stomach suddenly crimped with fear. Kevin hadn't been able to sufficiently maneuver his wheelchair, let alone walk. How would he get to an airport? How would he get anywhere?

"Hey, now, don't frown so hard." The corners of Brent's mouth turned upward in a small grin. "We'll find him. Could be that Mac flew into town and took Wink back to Houston with her."

Lara recalled Kevin's last phone call with the woman.

"Somehow, I don't think that's the case."

Brent smirked. "Well, you know, poor Wink's got a head injury."

"But he's not brain damaged."

Brent chuckled again, but Lara felt sick. She thought over every possible scenario, but none made sense.

She touched Brent's forearm, and he stopped discussing restaurants with Barb and Polly long enough for her to get a question in.

"Are you sure they didn't say Kevin was *transferred* to another floor or unit?"

"I was told *discharged*."

"That's impossible." Lara opened her purse and searched for her cell phone.

"Get in the van, Lara," Barb said. "We'll talk about it on the way to the restaurant. Brent, Austin, and few of the guys are riding in Brent's truck, so come on. . .we're all hungry.

"I want to call the hospital first. It'll only take a few minutes." Lara walked away from the van, across the gravel parking area until her phone registered a strong enough signal to place the call. She punched in County General's number, and soon the unit secretary answered her call.

"Hi, Kim, this is Lara Donahue, one of the social workers."

"Oh, yeah, hi, Lara."

"Hi. Say, listen, I'm calling about Kevin Wincouser."

"He was discharged yesterday."

"Discharged where?"

"To home, I guess. I don't know the ins and outs. You'd have to talk to his nurse."

"Okay, ask the RN if she's got a few minutes to talk to me."

The secretary acted a bit put out, but Lara was determined to find out Kevin's whereabouts. The nurse, however, didn't prove any more helpful.

"A friend came to get him," she said. "He almost checked out AMA, because apparently his insurance isn't picking up enough of his medical bills. But since Kevin promised to keep up his PT, the doctor ended up okaying the discharge."

"AMA?"

"Against medical advice."

"Oh, right." Lara was familiar with the terminology, but in her haste to find out Kevin's whereabouts, her mind momentarily went blank. "Was it a male or female friend who picked Kevin up?"

"Male."

Lara didn't have a clue as to who that friend could be. "All right. Well, thanks for the info."

Ending the call, she walked back to the van. She glanced around at her friends' curious expressions before she met Brent's keen stare.

"You're right. Kevin's been discharged from the hospital." She dropped her cell phone into her purse. "But it's anybody's guess where he went from there."

fifteen

Kevin stretched out on the soft double bed and stared across the room at a shelving unit, which held a row of picture frames: Ruthie, Tim, and Lara as kids, then as high school seniors, Ruthie's wedding picture, Tim's engagement photograph. Kevin wondered why Lara wasn't married. By now, she should at least have a steady boyfriend. She would make a great catch for a guy who wanted a wife and kids. Kevin had to chuckle to himself, however, when Tim said that his sister had a way of psychologically assessing her dates and finding them lacking in one area or another.

"Then it's a good thing I'm not dating her," Kevin had quipped. "She'd discover I'm a raving lunatic."

"I think Lara knows that already," Tim had shot right back.

Kevin's smile remained as he allowed his gaze to wander from the snapshots to a watercolor hanging on the wall on the right side of the bed. It depicted a church he found familiar. A second later, he realized it was the church he attended with his family before his parents were killed. The sight plucked a sad chord in his heart. On the lower right hand corner of the painting, it was signed "Ruth Ann Donahue, 1991."

She's a pretty good artist, Kevin decided. He had assumed the painting had been created by a professional. But in 1991, Ruthie had still been in high school.

And so had Kevin. He had graduated in 1993, one year after Ruthie.

At least my memory's intact. Unfortunately, all this time on his hands caused Kevin to remember more than he ever wanted.

He sighed and took in more of his surroundings. If he had to sum up the Donahues' guest bedroom in one word, it would be "homey." From the light blue walls to the fluffy blue carpet to the photos and paintings and the quilt on the bed, the entire room reminded Kevin of his family and brought back a sense of belonging. Indeed, it was a far cry from the trailer he shared with his buddies. Nothing "homey" about that place.

Kevin wondered if his head injury was causing him to become a sentimental fool, but his heart refuted the notion. There wasn't anything foolish about growing up and acting like a responsible human being, and maybe it was time Kevin grew up. If nothing else, these past weeks had taught him that a man needed a home, a place to which he could retreat when life assaulted him. Kevin's father had been fond of some such saying. What's more, had Dad been alive to witness Kevin's lifestyle over the last nine years, he would have likely disowned him. Dad wouldn't have put up with it, and Kevin realized he'd acted out his grief and anger by drinking and carousing.

Sadly enough, after all this time, the grief and anger still remained.

Lord, I'm not angry with You. I think I'm more angry with myself these days. . . .

A knock sounded, and the bedroom door opened revealing Tim's grinning face. "We're home from church, Kev. You okay?"

"Yeah, I just woke up a few minutes ago. What a lazy bum I am, eh?"

Tim opened the door wider and inched his lanky frame into the room. "I think springing you from the hospital yesterday took all your strength, then some."

"Yeah." Kevin had been stunned by his weakened condition.

"Well, Mom's in the kitchen making lunch. How 'bout I help you get dressed and into the living room. We can eat in there and watch the Brewers play baseball on TV?"

"I'd like that."

Kevin sat up and ran his fingers through his thick hair. It felt too long and shaggy, except for the bristly part on the left side, above his ear, where the doctors had shaved his head before surgery.

"I should probably get a haircut and even things out a bit." Kevin rubbed the left side of his head, and Tim chuckled.

"My dad could give you a military cut. I think I wore one every summer until my freshman year in high school."

Kevin grinned as he pulled on his jeans, remembering Tim's buzzed head. He tried not to feel impatient with his right hand. It felt stronger, but not up to par yet. "Wasn't your dad in the Navy or something?"

"Marines. He fought in Vietnam."

"That's right."

The chitchat ceased, and embarrassment engulfed Kevin when Tim had to assist him with zippers and buttons. Kevin felt like a two year old.

"Man, talk about a humbling experience."

Tim laughed. "Hey, don't worry about it. What are friends for?"

"Well, thanks."

Kevin realized he had never learned how to be a good friend. His focus had been on himself and on competing, winning, ever since he understood the concept of "Number One." Now, however, he couldn't imagine what he would have done without friends like the Donahues.

Kevin's spirit had hit an all-time low on the Fourth of July. Then Tim walked in, a veritable godsend. He had been on his way to his fiancée's house and decided to stop and say hello. A quick visit had turned into two hours of conversation that ended in heartfelt prayer. The next day, after learning about Kevin's financial dilemma, the Donahues offered him a place to recuperate. Less expensive—free, actually—and the food was a whole lot better.

Tim looped Kevin's right arm around his shoulders. "Ready?"

"As I'll ever be, I guess."

With Tim's help, Kevin managed to limp out of the bedroom and into the hallway. His right leg was weaker than his arm, although Kevin could stand now. But the signals from his brain to his leg muscles were still short-circuiting somewhere along the line.

Once more, Kevin feared he'd never rodeo again—a fate far worse than death for a two-time world bareback champion.

❧

Lara tried to hide her concern over the news that Kevin had left the hospital. She tried to pay attention to the light conversation during breakfast, but both Polly and Brent commented on how distracted she seemed. And it was true. But what bothered her most was the fact Kevin never even said good-bye. He only said he didn't want her help or her pity.

Perhaps, he hadn't planned to check himself out the last time they talked. Still, Lara couldn't help recalling how disheartened she felt the summer going into her sophomore year of high school when she learned Kevin had moved away.

She felt the same way now. Bummed out.

"Hey, will you cheer up over there?" Polly took the plastic straw out of her water glass and shook it at Lara.

The antic worked. Lara laughed, and moments later, she realized how silly she was to fret about a man and a situation over which she had no control. Taking a deep breath, she made the choice to turn her feelings over to the Lord.

Then, she listened in on Polly's conversation with Brent. The two sat next to each other, across from Lara at the long rectangular table, and they were discussing childhood pets, of all things. Minutes later, Lara's melancholy vanished, and she set aside all thoughts of Kevin and his disappearing act—until she arrived home that evening, and Tim met her at the curb.

"Hey, Sis, we've got company."

"You came to warn me?" Lara grinned.

"Well, yeah, sorta."

Lara allowed her brother to retrieve her luggage from the back of the minivan. After a wave to Polly and the others, she followed him to the side door of their duplex.

"Kevin moved in with us."

"He did *what*?" Incredulousness pervaded Lara's being, and as Tim spilled the story, everything made sense. "I think Kevin had better telephone his buddies and let them know where he is. They're worried. Brent tried to call him this morning."

"I'll pass that message along." Tim opened the door. "But I wanted to give you a heads-up so you don't come down in your nightgown and robe with a head full of curlers. Kevin never had sisters, you know."

"Oh, so you're worried that I'll scare him, huh?"

"Likely so."

Lara gave Tim a sisterly shove. "Oh, hush."

He chuckled in reply before taking the stairs to the second floor two at a time. Lara passed him on the steps as he ran back down.

"Your suitcase is in the hallway," he said. "Come visit later."

"Yeah, with my hair in rollers."

She laughed and entered the flat she shared with her grandmother. The easy banter with Tim helped the shock to wear off. But now disbelief took its place.

Kevin is here? In my parents' house? He and I are under the same roof?

Well, one thing was certain; Lara wouldn't be stupid twice. She would keep her distance. She'd keep her thoughts to herself and wouldn't offer any assistance, unless Kevin asked, of course.

"Lara, I'm down here." Gram's voice wafted up the back stairwell. "We're having supper. Come and join us."

"I ate already. Thanks anyway. Tell Mom and Dad I'll stop in later."

A nervous flutter filled her abdomen. Why did she feel suddenly doomed?

sixteen

"Wink, you dirty dog, you broke her heart."

Sitting on the Donahues' wide front porch, Kevin sighed as Brent railed on him for hurting Lara's feelings three days ago.

"Look, I didn't mean any harm. I'm going through a tough time right now. Doctors say I'll never ride again, and I'm trying to prove them wrong. Lara understands."

"Sure she does."

"I'll apologize, and she'll forgive me." Kevin shifted in the plastic lawn chair. He wasn't very comfortable out here with the mosquitoes and humidity, but his cell phone had better reception outdoors than in the house.

"Well, you're right about that. Lara will forgive you." Brent's voice sounded strained as though he were in the process of reclining. Then he exhaled. "We had a nice time this weekend. All of us. There were seven women to about four of us guys. Great odds, wouldn't you say?"

Kevin grinned in spite of himself. "Yeah."

"On Saturday, Lara and I danced the night away."

"Is that right?" Kevin wondered why he felt tense all of a sudden. On second thought, he knew the reason. He didn't want Lara to get hurt as a result of Brent's vengeance. But he wouldn't let on that the remark troubled him. If he did, Brent was liable to continue his spiteful game. "Glad you had fun. You deserve it."

"Yeah, I guess I do. It's been a while since I had good clean fun." Brent chuckled as if he suddenly recalled something amusing. "Have you met Lara's friend Polly?"

"Once, I think."

"She's a hoot. Pretty too."

"Yeah?"

"Yeah. Lara says she's interested in me, but. . .I just don't see it."

"Lara's interested in you? She said that?"

"No, no. Lara said *Polly* is interested in me."

"Oh, gotcha." Kevin hoped he didn't sound as relieved as he felt. Then he remembered Lara mentioning her friend's "crush."

"I guess I knew that."

"Anyway, Polly doesn't act interested, so it kind of confuses a guy. Know what I mean?"

"It's a gender thing. Women have confounded us since the Garden of Eden."

"How do you know?"

"Um, I've read a lot of books."

Brent let go of a hearty belly laugh. "Wink, I'll eat buffalo chips for a week if you've read a book in the last five years."

"Yeah, well, good thing for you I can't recall the last book I picked up." Kevin chuckled. He was beginning to enjoy conversing with his pal.

They chatted for a while longer, exchanging occasional barbs, then discussed current rodeo standings. Finally, Kevin felt himself growing stiff and told Brent he'd call back in a couple of days. Turning off his phone, Kevin had just slipped it into his shirt pocket when a soft, female voice drifted down from somewhere up above, although her words belied her tone.

"Your friend is a fibber."

Fibber? Kevin twisted around and saw Lara perched on the upstairs porch railing. With the moon directly behind her and her hair hanging down past her shoulders, she made a fetching sight.

"What are you doing up there? Eavesdropping?"

"Yes, except I didn't mean to."

Kevin grinned. That girl was honest to a fault. With some effort, he managed to turn his chair around far enough so he didn't have to crane his neck to look at her. The upper porch wasn't even half the size of the deck and it only covered the two front doors, as if its original purpose was to protect arriving guests from the elements.

But obviously, it had other uses too.

"I was here when Tim helped you out of the house and into the lawn chair," Lara explained. "I didn't think there was any reason for me to go in. But then you started talking and I realized you were on your cell phone. By that time, there was no way for me to make a graceful exit."

"Okay. No harm done." Kevin wasn't offended in the least. "So what did Brent *fib* about?"

"I'm not interested in him."

"Well, see? You've got it wrong already. I was the one who misunderstood. Brent explained that it's Polly who's got stars in her eyes." *And you've got the moon in your hair,* he thought, feeling oddly captivated.

Lara bent her legs so that she could wrap her arms around her knees. Her back was up against the front of the house.

"Why don't you come on down here so we can talk?" Kevin cajoled. "You can tell me what else Brent's lying about."

Lara didn't move, and Kevin wondered if she was thinking over his offer.

Then he remembered. . .

"Hey, look, I'm really sorry about what I said to you on Thursday afternoon."

"Oh, yes, that's right. You said you'd apologize, and you were very confident that I'd forgive you."

"Of course you'll forgive me. You're a good Christian girl."

Kevin couldn't see her features in the darkness, but he imagined she had pursed her lips in an effort to stave off a grin and had raised one pretty eyebrow. That look was her habitual expression to weak retorts, and Kevin felt a little amazed that he even knew something like that about her. "Come on down here, Lara. Keep me company for awhile."

Once again, she didn't move nor did she reply. Kevin figured she was still miffed, so he tried a new approach.

"You know, just like you didn't intend to listen in on my *private conversation*, I didn't intend to hurt your feelings. I took out my frustration on you, and that was wrong. I regretted it the instant you left my hospital room. Now, are you going to forgive me, or not?"

"Yes, I forgive you."

"Good." Kevin smiled with satisfaction. "Now, come down here."

"I can talk to you from where I am."

Kevin thought it over. "Did Brent tell you to be careful around me? If he did, I'm here to say that I'm harmless. More so than dancing with *him* all night, that's for sure!"

"What?"

"Yeah, you heard me. Brent said the two of you 'danced the night away' on Saturday."

Lara started to laugh so hard that Kevin feared she'd fall from her perch. If that happened, he'd be unable to come to her rescue, and the realization made him feel all the more useless.

"You're making me nervous," he barked. "Get off that banister."

Lara did as he said, then entered the house and closed the porch door behind her. As the minutes ticked by, Kevin started to think she wasn't coming out, and the disappointment he felt surprised him. Well, what did he expect? He shouldn't have used such a harsh tone with her. But he hated feeling so inadequate. On the other hand, everyone kept telling him to be patient.

Suddenly, he heard a rustling of the bushes, then footfalls on the wooden front porch steps. Moments later, Lara appeared carrying a large candle. She'd come from around the side of the house.

"Where were you?"

"In the backyard. I stopped to pick up this candle from off the picnic table. It's supposed to keep the bugs away." She struck a match, and a golden hue spread across the porch.

Kevin found the soft light rather romantic, although his practical side hoped the candle proved effective on the bugs. The mosquitoes were eating him alive. He slapped at one on his right arm, then looked over at Lara. She stared back with a curious expression.

"What's wrong?"

"Did you get your hair cut?"

Kevin chuckled. "Yep. The top of my head feels like a tennis ball."

"Must be my dad's handiwork."

"You got it."

A tiny laugh escaped Lara.

Kevin smiled. "Now, about this dancing business. . ."

"One dance. And I didn't even enjoy it."

"No?" Kevin was glad to hear that. "How come?"

"Because, well, I felt uncomfortable." Lara tucked one leg beneath her. "I mean, if Brent were the guy I vowed to spend the rest of my life with, it might be different. But he's not, so such close, personal contact didn't seem right to me. But I suppose I had to learn that lesson firsthand."

"Hmm."

"I sound like a prude, right? Well, maybe I am."

"I take it we're not talking about line dancing here, are we?" The sound of Lara's laughter made Kevin chuckle.

"Lara, Lara, Lara." He said her name on a long sigh, a feigned reprimand. "Dancing with the cowboys. What are we going to do with you?"

"Shhh." She put her forefinger to her lips. "I don't want my parents to hear. They'll lock me in my room until I'm thirty!"

Kevin grinned, but he felt sure the Donahues weren't at all *lock-her-up* type of people. They were bighearted folks with a wealth of compassion.

And they'd raised a proper, upstanding daughter who wasn't at all a "prude." In fact, Kevin found her...*refreshing*.

❧

The month of July passed in a busy blur at work for Lara, mostly because her heart was at home. She had become accustomed to seeing Kevin around, and even though she reminded herself to keep her distance—to keep her emotions detached from him and his situation—it didn't help. She always ended up sitting on the porch with him, talking and watching the sunset, or just watching TV with him and her parents.

Mike Donahue, Lara's father, had taken Kev under his wing, so to speak. He drove him to and from physical therapy sessions and assisted Kevin with his exercises at home.

"Mike's Boot Camp for Lame Cowboys," Kevin called it in jest, but he showed obvious signs of improvement. Kevin could walk using an aluminum "elbow crutch," one that fit securely around his upper arm for maximum stability. His speech sounded better, although he still had problems with detailed tasks, such as buttoning a shirt and writing.

Lara's mother had the summer off from her part-time teaching position, so she took pride in cooking, baking, and tending to her small "urban garden." Everyone benefited from Peg Donahue's domesticity; however, Kevin seemed to thrive on it, much to Peg's delight.

For weeks, everything appeared to be progressing at a nice, even pace, until Kevin learned from Quincy that Mackenzie Sabino had plans to sue him for breach of contract. The news troubled Kevin. In addition to rising medical bills, it depressed him to think he'd have to hire an attorney to defend him in court. However, Mike Donahue stepped in and contacted a lawyer he knew from church. After hearing the scenario, the advocate surmised that Mac and her daddy's salsa company didn't have much of a case, given the fact that Kevin had been injured through no fault of his own.

The news brought Kevin a small measure of relief, but he told Lara that, knowing Mac, she'd try to get back at him some other way.

August arrived bringing with it the hot, sticky temperatures. Lara found herself seeking out Kevin's company, yet in spite of the handsome distraction at home, Lara continued her volunteer work at The Regeneration Ranch. She had missed the first Saturday in July, due to the holiday. But two weeks later, she spent an entire day with her kids and enjoyed every minute of it. By Lara's first scheduled weekend in August, Kevin was hobbling around well enough that she asked him to go along to the ranch with her. He accepted the offer, and Lara worked out all the details with the ranch personnel. Her kids would finally meet a real rodeo star!

"I can't believe you won't come to Iowa with me," Polly whined on Friday afternoon. It was the day before Kevin's grand appearance at the ranch. A mini-rodeo followed by a picnic had been planned.

At her friend's complaint, Lara didn't even pause in cleaning off her desk for the weekend. Polly knew where she stood. Lara refused the offer to attend this weekend's rodeo and wasn't about to change her mind.

"Since last week when Brent called me, I've really wanted to go."

"I know." Lara recalled how excited her friend had been after Brent's phone call. The two of them shared what Polly termed "a meaningful conversation."

"I want to see him again. I think he might really be *the one.*"

Lara cast an exasperated glance toward the ceiling.

"Please, come with me."

"Take Annmarie."

"Yeah, looks like I'll have to."

Grinning at Polly's cynical tone, Lara stuffed her leather folder and other paperwork into a drawer and locked it. "You guys will have a great time."

"You really won't come?"

"No, and I told you before, I enjoy watching the rodeo, but I don't care for what goes on behind the scenes."

"Well, I don't, either, but I care about Brent."

"So Austin's out of the picture for good, eh?"

Polly shrugged. "He only e-mailed me once, and I haven't heard from him since." She tipped her head. "But you and Kevin are certainly hitting it off nicely."

"We're friends."

"Oh, Lara, you are *so* in denial."

She laughed and stepped out of her office. The second-shift social worker had taken over, and it was time for Lara to punch out—and time for Polly to get back to work.

"Listen, it's true. Kevin and I are just friends. I'll admit I wish it were more, but he still talks about rodeoing again. He's determined to return to the circuit a changed man, in more ways than one."

Lara grabbed her purse before she and Polly ambled through

the emergency department, past the trauma room, and down the hallway to the time clock.

"It's great that Kevin's been attending church with your family." Polly pulled a stick of gum from out of the pocket of her multicolored smock-top. "Brent hasn't been quite as faithful, but he's been going from time to time."

Lara's heart thrilled at the news. "Kevin's talked to him about the Lord too."

"We've made a difference in these guys' lives," Polly said. "Nothing more might develop between us in the way of romantic relationships, but God used us to bring them closer to Him. And that's what this life is all about for Christians, isn't it?"

"Yep." Smiling, Lara swiped her badge through the automated time-tracking device on the wall. Then she swung around and gave Polly a hug. "Have fun this weekend, okay?"

"I'll try, but it won't be the same without you."

Lara caught Polly's simulated pout before her friend turned on her heel and walked toward the elevators. With a smile still on her lips, Lara headed for the parking lot, feeling excited about everything that God had done. And everything He was about to do.

seventeen

On Saturday morning, Lara bounded down the back steps with anticipation flowing through her veins. Today was the big day at The Regeneration Ranch. She just knew her kids were going to be so excited!

Turning the corner on the landing, she proceeded down the next set of stairs only to come face-to-face with a very unhappy-looking Kevin Wincouser. He stood just outside her parents' back doorway wearing faded blue jeans, a short-sleeved blue and white shirt whose bold stripes ran vertically, and a heavy frown.

"What's wrong?"

"Me. That's what's wrong." He lifted his right hand, indicating the crutch he held. "How am I supposed to impress a bunch of kids today?"

"These kids will be impressed. Believe me."

"Lara, I had to wake up Tim and ask him to button my shirt this morning."

She wondered if he worried about finding assistance at the ranch should he require it. "There will be men around who can help you today if you need it."

"I hadn't even thought about that." He groaned.

Lara took a step toward him. "I wouldn't have asked you to come today if I didn't think you could manage. Once we get to the ranch, you'll see what I mean."

Kevin didn't look convinced.

Dropping her shoulder bag onto the steps, Lara reached for his left hand and held it between both of hers. "Please don't change your mind. My kids will be so disappointed. So will I."

"Why? I'm like damaged goods. There are other cowboys in Wisconsin, some that could entertain *your kids* with roping tricks or even a bull ride. I'm sure they'd do it for free too. Brent, Quincy, and I made charity appearances once in awhile."

"But we want *you*. I've talked about you, and my kids want to meet the guy who was my hero when I was thirteen."

"Was. That's a good word to describe me." His blue eyes looked misty, and the sight broke Lara's heart.

"Kevin, you have so much to offer. I wish you'd see that." She smiled. "And just for the record, you're still my hero."

He raised his brows, and a hint of a grin tugged at his mouth. "Lara Donahue, are you flirting with me?"

She managed to contain a smile. "Well, maybe just a little."

He twisted out of her grasp, and within moments, his arm encircled her waist, and he pulled her up next to him. "A girl could get in big trouble flirting like that."

"You're right. She could." Lara stood so close to him that she smelled the mint on his breath and the spicy scent of his cologne.

Kevin narrowed his gaze. "She could even get kissed."

"Well, it's about time!"

His eyes widened with surprise, and Lara laughed.

"I've only been waiting twelve years for you to kiss me." She said it in jest, but her heart had told the truth.

"Why didn't you say something sooner? I'm more than happy to oblige."

She laughed again, but very suddenly, it wasn't funny anymore. Kevin's eyes darkened to cobalt, and an ardent expression crossed his features. The seconds that followed were a million times more romantic than anything Lara had ever experienced, not that she possessed a wealth of knowledge in this particular area. But the instant his lips touched hers, she knew she loved Kevin. In fact, she had probably loved him for half her life.

The kiss ended, and Lara felt oddly disappointed.

"We'd better, um, get going," Kevin stammered. "I mean, folks at the ranch are most likely waiting for us."

"Right."

Kevin released her, and Lara forced her legs backwards. She grabbed her shoulder bag and followed Kevin, who had already managed to descend the three steps leading to the outer doorway.

In the car, as Lara drove to the ranch, neither she nor Kevin spoke. The silence told Lara a single kiss had altered their friendship. But why? It couldn't have meant anything to him. Surely, he'd kissed a dozen women in his lifetime. Maybe more. But, perhaps, that was the problem. Lara's kiss hadn't measured up to his expectations. Should she apologize?

❧

Kevin didn't know what to say. Kissing Lara had activated every neuron in his brain, and now his thoughts were in a jumble. Talk about electric currents! That kiss could have lit up Chicago at Christmastime! He stole a glance in her direction. Had she felt it too?

Lara braked for a stoplight, and Kevin brought his gaze forward. *So now what do I do, Lord? I'm going to fall for this woman, and then what? I leave her? Break her heart?*

Kevin couldn't stand the thought of hurting Lara. *I could take her with me. Marry her. . .* Kevin shook his head, trying to clear his thoughts. *What am I thinking?* He couldn't believe he actually considered "tying the knot." He had successfully dodged wedding bells for twenty-nine years. Besides, marrying Lara wouldn't work. She had already expressed her aversion to his lifestyle.

Former lifestyle. *That's right, Lord, I've recommitted my ways to You.*

The light changed, and Lara stepped on the accelerator.

"Kevin, I can't stand it anymore. I'm sorry if I offended you."

He looked over at her. "What?"

"You know. What happened before. . .I'm sorry."

"Why are you sorry?"

"Because. . ." She swallowed hard, and her voice sounded strained. It dawned on Kevin that she might be upset. "Because you're not talking to me."

"Sure, I'm talking to you. I just don't have anything to say at the moment." Clutching the steering wheel with her right hand, she lifted her left and proceeded to swat at something on her cheek. Kevin felt like the dumbest mule in the stable. He'd somehow hurt her feelings. "Lara, you're not crying, are you?"

She skirted his question. "I just don't want you to be angry with me."

Kevin chuckled. "I'm not angry. Never was."

"When you didn't say anything, I thought I did something wrong."

"No-oo." Kevin reached out his hand, and she took it so fast it made him grin. "Lara, I'll be honest. I'm developing strong feelings for you, and I'm not sure what to do about them. Seems like we're from two different worlds, and I'm not talking about Venus and Mars, either."

She laughed, and the sound made Kevin smile.

"That's better. No more tears now, you hear? It sort of rips me apart inside to see you sad."

She took her gaze off the road for the briefest of moments, and although Kevin couldn't read the message in her eyes through the dark sunglasses she wore, he did see her smile.

And that was good enough. For now.

æ

Sitting in the bleachers, Lara watched the mini-rodeo with her kids and several parents. The "rodeo" consisted of an opening act with two funny clowns who looked suspiciously like Caroline and Ron Bramble, the owners of the ranch. But the kids didn't seem to notice, and they laughed at the silly antics.

Next, a mechanical bull was placed in the center of the corral, and several of the older kids who had been practicing for weeks got to show off their skills. Not a one fell off, either. Of course, the bull's speed had been set so low its riders appeared to be in slow motion. Nevertheless, it was a miracle to watch, given the children's physical disabilities.

Finally, Kevin "Wink" Wincouser rode into the corral on poor old Abby, an ebony-maned, chestnut brown mare that probably couldn't even trot anymore, let alone buck off a cowboy. But since Kevin was in no condition for bronc riding, Abby would do just fine. Horse and rider circled the pen once while Kevin waved to the kids. They cheered and clapped. Then, reining in the animal, Kevin stopped and faced his audience. Next, he pulled his crutch from behind the saddle as though it were a shiny, sliver saber and held it up for all to see.

That's my hero, Lara thought with a smile. Kevin's words from this morning still played in her heart. She tried not to think of forever but forced herself instead to place the matter in God's hands.

And leave it there.

Kevin began to explain why he had to walk with a crutch. He talked about his head injury and admitted it was by God's grace and mercy that he was able to climb back up in the saddle today.

"See, I'm not so different from any of you kids."

Lara grinned, thinking Kevin had unwittingly just endeared himself to the children around her. It was obvious that he had a dynamic way of speaking to youngsters, and Lara felt proud of him.

"And here's something else you should know about me. When I was a little boy, I dreamed of becoming a real live cowboy. Some people told me I'd never make it. Some people even laughed at me."

"That's mean to laugh at other people," eight-year-old Jason Emory whispered to Lara with his adorable lisp.

She nodded. Jason knew firsthand how it felt to be mocked. He had severe learning disabilities, and sometimes the kids at his school picked on him.

"But I worked really hard, and each time I fell down," Kevin said, "I picked myself right back up. I refused to give up. And none of you should give up, either. Now, who wants to learn how to ride a horse?"

Lara laughed as practically every hand around her shot up.

"Well, then, you'd better get down here in a hurry and form a single line by the gate over there. I'm going to give you each a special riding lesson."

The kids whooped with excitement, and even though many of them had already ridden astride Abby, none had ever received a lesson from a real rodeo cowboy.

Lined up against the split-rail fence, the children wiggled and waited none-too-patiently for their turns. Parents who brought cameras snapped pictures of their son or daughter getting a tip from Kevin.

Then, suddenly, Lara spotted Maria Kallen at the head of the line. Jogging over to reach her, Lara caught the small girl by the hand.

"I don't think you want a turn, Sweetie." Lara knew the seven year old was frightened of the animals even though she admired them from afar and often talked about the day when she'd ride a horse.

"Yes, I do. I want to ride."

Lara caught sight of the determined expression on Maria's face and decided to let her try. In the past, the towheaded girl came as close as a foot away from a horse before she panicked. Part of the problem, Lara knew, was the child's poor eyesight.

"Come on, Honey. You're next."

Maria's cheeks turned a pretty pink.

Cowboy charm affects females of all ages, Lara thought with a smirk as the child shyly stepped forward.

But just as Lara predicted, the girl got about two feet away and changed her mind.

"Whoa, now, don't run away." Kevin leaned over and halted Maria by taking hold of her arm. Kneeling, using his good leg, he rested his forearm on his right thigh. "You're not scared, are you?"

Lara watched Maria nod out a silent reply.

"Well, I'll tell you what. How 'bout I set you in the saddle first, then I'll climb up behind you? Nothing bad will happen if I'm hanging onto you."

To Lara's astonishment, the girl agreed.

Kevin stood and gently hoisted Maria into the worn, brown leather saddle before mounting the horse. The two then took a leisurely amble around the corral. Kevin even let Maria hold the reins. When they rounded the last bend, Lara took one glance at the expression of sheer delight on the little girl's face and had to fight back tears of joy. The child was living her very own dream come true.

"I'm riding! I'm riding!" Maria squealed. Her large blue eyes seemed magnified behind the clear, plastic-framed glasses she wore.

"Great job, Maria," Kevin told her after their ride ended.

"You're a bona fide cowgirl now." He lifted her off the saddle and placed the child into Lara's outstretched arms.

"I did it, Miss Lara! I did it!"

"Yes, you did." She set the child onto the ground.

Maria skipped away. "I did it! I did it!"

"And I didn't have my video camera," Lara muttered, feeling disappointed.

"Guess we'll have to bring it next time."

We? Lara raised an inquiring brow. "Does that mean you're coming back to the ranch with me in the near future?"

"Oh, I dunno." Kevin leaned forward in the saddle. "I could probably be persuaded."

Smiling, Lara glimpsed the mischievous spark in his blue eyes and decided she might like to take him up on the challenge.

"Hey! Is it my turn now?" A child's voice interrupted.

Lara blinked, and Kevin straightened in the saddle. Dismounting, he was careful to pull his left foot out of the stirrup before he landed.

"Guess you and I will have to finish this discussion later." A note of promise rang in his tone.

"Guess so." Lara couldn't wait. But for now her kids took priority. She glanced at Billy Stievers, the next child in line, and waved him over.

eighteen

After the riding lessons and picnic, Lara helped Caroline Bramble and several other volunteers pick up garbage. Tying one of the trash bags, Lara happened to glance at the gray and white barn off in the distance and spotted Kevin, leaning against the doorframe and talking with Ron. They appeared to be deep in conversation, and Lara wondered what they were talking about.

Ron is probably "persuading" Kevin to volunteer here at the ranch. Lara grinned at the thought. Ron Bramble was a lot more influential than she, although she might have enjoyed giving it a try in Kevin's case.

Once the yard was free of litter, Lara followed Caroline into their large house. The outside of the dwelling matched the barn, and inside, the home looked cozy. The yellow and white kitchen was large, and a vase of daisies sat in the center of the round, wooden table. Crocheted afghan blankets covered the backs of the sofa and love seat in the "parlor." Walls everywhere were decorated with snapshots and drawings, given to Ron and Caroline by children who had benefited from the ranch's ministry over the last twenty-four years. In all, it was a very special place.

Lara accepted the can of cola Caroline offered her. Popping its flip-top, she took a long drink. She hadn't stopped all day, and suddenly, she realized how exhausted she felt. Minutes later, Kevin and Ron entered the house, and Lara sensed Kevin was equally as tired.

"I s'pose we should be on our way," Lara said, with a glance in Kev's direction.

He nodded, obviously ready to go.

They bid farewell to the Brambles, then made their way to Lara's car. Once seated and buckled in, they sighed in unison and leaned against the backs of the front seats.

"This is more excitement than I'm used to."

Lara looked over at Kevin and smiled. "I'm sure you're right. I just hope you didn't overdo it today." She bit her lower lip, realizing her blunder. "Sorry, Kevin, I didn't mean to sound motherly."

"That's okay." He gave her a wink. "I think I'm getting used to it."

She expelled a breath of indignation before laughing and rapping Kevin in the arm for the quip.

On the drive home, they chatted about the day's events. Lara commended Kevin on a job well done.

"You know, Lara, it's an odd thing, but when I got on that horse today, I just knew I'd never rodeo again."

"What?" She took her eyes off the road long enough to send Kevin a stunned look. "I can't believe I just heard those words come out of your mouth."

"Well, you did. Part of me feels like I just learned my best friend died, while another part of me is relieved. I mean, I'm retiring a two-time world champion bareback rider. It's not like I'm going out a loser."

"Certainly not a loser."

As she further digested his news, Lara didn't know what more to say. Like Kevin, she had mixed emotions. On one hand, she felt elated that he had decided not to rodeo. It meant he wouldn't get reinjured, and maybe there was really hope for a budding romance between them. But she also knew it was a hard decision for Kevin to make.

"You were great with the kids today," she murmured. It had nothing to do with the present topic, but she couldn't seem to tell him that enough.

"Thanks. Ron thought so too. He offered me a job."

"You're kidding?"

"Nope. And it's actually not a bad paying position, either. But the salary is probably only half what I'd earn in this year competing."

"What would you be doing at the ranch?"

"Probably anything and everything I'm physically able to do. We didn't get into a lot of specifics. I told Ron I'd give the matter some thought—and, of course, I need to ask God what He thinks."

Lara smiled to herself. Two months ago, praying about a situation wouldn't have occurred to Kevin. He'd come a long way, spiritually and physically.

Their conversation lagged, and Lara felt tempted to ask Kevin what he thought about *them*. Was he interested in pursuing a relationship? However, Lara sensed now wasn't a good time to talk romance. Kevin looked tired, and his thoughts were obviously stayed on one of the biggest decisions he ever faced.

She exhaled and, once again, set the matter in her Savior's hands.

&

As the month progressed, plans for Tim and Amanda's wedding took precedence. October fourth, their special day, was creeping ever nearer. Lara had a final fitting for her bridesmaid's dress, and being the groom's sister, she helped coordinate Amanda's bridal shower. To make life all the busier, one of the three social workers quit at the hospital, and Lara and her coworker were forced to divide the job between them until another person could be hired and trained. There didn't seem to be much time for budding romances, especially since Ron had moved Kevin into the apartment above the barn on The Regeneration Ranch. One evening, Lara came downstairs to say hello, and her father gave her the "good news."

Little did he know the information caused his daughter's heart to crimp in misery. But Lara reminded herself that Kevin hadn't made her any promises. When two weeks passed and she didn't see him at church, nor did he call, Lara began to think she had imagined the kiss they'd shared as well as the conversation following it. Perhaps she'd somehow misunderstood when Kevin said he was "developing strong feelings" for her. Of course, he had added that he didn't know what do to about them. Maybe he decided they weren't worth pursuing.

"Are you going to our singles' group meeting tonight?" Polly asked on that first Friday evening of September.

Lara held the phone between her ear and shoulder while she arranged an assortment of vegetables on a relish tray for Amanda's shower the next day. "No, I've got too much to do."

"I'm not going, either. I just don't feel like it."

Deciding to take a break, Lara went to the freezer and lopped out two hearty scoops of chocolate ice cream. Then she took the plastic dish and portable phone outside on the little porch off of the living room. Summer was still in the air, even though Back-To-School sales raged on at all the local discount stores. Lara's mother had already returned to her part-time teaching position.

"So any news from Kevin?"

"No." Lara spooned a bite of ice cream into her mouth. "How 'bout you? Heard from Brent?"

"No."

She swallowed. "What is with these guys? Don't they know two awesome women when they meet them?"

"I take it you're referring to us? You and me? The two awesome women?"

Lara laughed. "Who else would I be talking about?"

"Well, I wanted to clarify things. . ."

Again, Lara laughed. She thanked God for a friend like Polly who could always find humor in every situation.

"Amanda looks like a fairy princess in her wedding dress," Lara said. "Wait until you see her."

"I'm sure I'll wish it were me walking down the aisle."

"I already wish it were me."

"Hey, I've got an idea. What if we go ahead and start planning our own weddings and just trust God to provide the grooms?"

"Yeah, right." Despite the sarcastic reply, Lara smiled and took another bite of ice cream.

"I'm serious. We trust God for everything else, right? Food, clothing, finances. Why not this area?"

"We are trusting God in this area. But we're supposed to know our grooms before we marry them. The other way around is like putting the cart before the horse."

"No, it isn't. It's stepping out in faith."

Lara laughed. Her friend was such a goof.

"When do you want to get married? Winter? Spring? Summer? Fall?"

"I don't care," Lara quipped. "ASAP."

"What's the rush? It can take *years* to plan a wedding."

"I suppose it could. But if Kevin proposed to me tonight, I'd marry him tomorrow."

"Oh, Lara, really!" Polly lowered her voice and drawled, sounding like a rich, eccentric, great aunt. "The perfect wedding takes time to plan. Don't you read the bridal magazines?"

❧

Kevin was hard-pressed not to hoot as he and Tim stood directly beneath the porch on which Lara sat. He'd just ambled up the front walk with Tim, and Lara never heard their arrival.

"At least I know she'd say 'yes' if I ever asked." He whispered the remark so Lara wouldn't hear.

"Don't do it, Kev," Tim whispered back. "You haven't seen my sister with her hair in curlers and green goop smeared all over her face. She looks like she's from outer space."

Kevin chuckled under his breath.

"Once a little brother, always a little brother. That's me."

"Shhh. . ."

"Sorry," Tim whispered back.

"This here's payback time." Kevin grinned, recalling how Lara had inadvertently eavesdropped on him. "I think I'll sneak up there and surprise her." He glanced at his watch, barely able to make out the Roman numerals in the darkness. "I think we've got some time, don't we?"

"About a half-hour. Clayt's plane doesn't get in until eight-fifty-five, and when I called it was running on time."

"Okay, I'll see you in thirty minutes."

"Right."

Kevin did his best not to make a sound as he entered the Donahues' lower flat. He made his way back through the empty living room, wondering where Mike was tonight. As he walked into the dining room, he could hear Lara's mother and grandmother discussing something in the master bedroom, and he got the impression the two ladies were discussing wedding particulars and the dresses they had purchased for Tim's big day.

Making his way upstairs without the aid of his crutch, Kevin tried not to let the old wooden steps creak beneath his weight. But he needn't have worried that Lara would hear his approach because as he snuck into the upper flat, she was laughing so hard she wouldn't have heard a door slam, let alone footfalls in the stairwell.

Even so, Kevin moved noiselessly through the living room

until he came to the screened porch door. Because of the lighting in the house, Kevin knew Lara would be able to see him much better than he could her, so he leaned on the doorframe and folded his arms as though he'd been standing there for hours.

"No, Polly, don't choose that color. I don't look good in pinks," Lara paused as if listening to the reply. "Oh, yeah, that's right. By the time *you* get married, I'll be expecting my eighth child."

Kevin winced. Lara didn't really want eight kids, did she?

"I'm not a betting woman." Lara rose from her chair. "Besides, you're probably right. The way my life is going, you just might get married before me."

At that instant, Lara glanced at Kevin in the doorway and shrieked.

He laughed.

"Polly, I have to go. I'll call you later."

"I'd love to be listening in on that next conversation." He chuckled again.

Kevin stepped back as Lara yanked the door open and marched into the house.

She glared at him. "What are you doing here?!"

"It's nice to see you too. Say, did you know that when you're angry, your eyes take on a real pretty shade of green?"

Lara narrowed her gaze. "Don't try to charm me, Kevin Wincouser. How long were you standing there?"

"Oh. . ." He made like he had to think about it. "Long enough to be in on the wedding plans."

At Lara's little yelp of indignation, Kevin laughed again—until she stormed toward him.

"Now, Lara."

She grabbed both sides of his shirt and clutched it in her fists. "You've got a lot of nerve showing up out of nowhere and listening to my private conversation with Polly."

"Are you really mad at me?" Kevin couldn't believe it. "It was all in fun, and since you were discussing *our wedding*—"

"What I was or wasn't discussing is no—"

Kevin kissed her, figuring that would take the wind out of her sails.

He was right.

Slipping his arms around her waist, he realized how much he'd missed her.

"Want to come to the airport with me? I asked Tim if he'd drive."

"Are you leaving?"

"No." Kevin watched as a look of relief spread across her features, and he realized she truly loved him. Lots of women had said they loved him, but he'd never seen the emotion staring back at him like he did now as he gazed into Lara's face. The sight endeared her to him all the more. Holding her closer, he rested his cheek against her forehead.

"What do you have to go to the airport for?"

"Hmm? Oh."

For a moment, Kevin had lost all track of his thoughts. But that's what this woman did to him. Skewed his senses. Made him think about marriage, a home, and even raising a family of his own—everything he'd avoided and even condemned for the last decade.

Collecting his wits, he answered Lara's question. "Clayt and I have been talking. We've sort of patched things up between us, and now he and his wife and my four-month-old nephew are flying into Milwaukee so we can have a long overdue family reunion."

"That's terrific!" Lara pulled back and smiled.

"I figured you'd approve."

"I do."

Kevin smirked. "Was that a practice?"

It took a moment, then she caught his meaning. "Oh, you!" Pushing away from him, Lara whirled around and stomped her way down the hallway.

He chuckled, thinking she was awfully cute when she was mad. "Hey, are you coming with me, or not?"

"Yes. Let me get my purse."

nineteen

A muggy autumn breeze tousled Lara's hair and clothing as, one week later, she climbed out of her car and traipsed across the wide-open yard at The Regeneration Ranch. She hadn't seen or heard from Kevin since last Friday night. But it appeared that he and Clayt were well on their way to repairing their brotherly relationship, except Lara didn't know for sure. She'd been occupied with Amanda's shower the next day, and for the past month, Kevin had been attending a Bible study and church service with the Brambles so she hadn't seen him on Sunday. Then they both worked all week long, and as a result, Lara never did learn the final results of the Wincouser reunion.

And what about us? Kevin could have called me.

In all her confusion over where she stood with him, Lara bristled. According to Polly, Brent phoned her at least once a week, and they talked for hours.

Kevin and I live in the same city. A date would be nice. He's not exactly broke.

Regarding the latter, Lara had to admit she didn't really know his financial situation, although she suspected it wasn't as desperate as Kevin first imagined. He'd told her the financial counselor at County General had worked out a payment plan and even reduced his out-of-pocket costs because he agreed to pay a bulk of the debt up front.

He could at least afford a pizza for two.

She stomped into the barn, and suspecting Kevin was lurking about, she purposely strode past the office without a glance and headed for the corral where her kids were congregating.

"Hey!"

Kevin's voice hailed her, but she kept on walking.

"I thought that was you. Lara! Aren't you even going to stop and say good morning?"

She paused, remembering The Golden Rule. Pivoting, she manufactured a smile. "Good morning, Kevin." Whirling back around, she continued on her way.

"Um, s'cuse me."

"Yes?" Lara turned to face him again.

"Is something wrong?"

She tipped her head. "What could be wrong?"

Placing his right hand on the wooden edging below the office window, Kevin moved toward her. His limp seemed more pronounced today and watching him hobble toward her lessened her annoyance.

"Well, I dunno, but I've been looking forward to seeing you today, and I guess I expected a little warmer greeting."

Lara took a few steps toward him. "If you want to have a relationship with me, you're going to have to put forth a little effort. When I don't hear from you for an entire week, I start to think you don't care."

"Look, I've been busy. My motor's running from sunup to sunset, and after I eat supper, I usually pass out from exhaustion. Sometimes I never even bother to change clothes. One day last week, I slept with my boots on. That's how tired I was."

While Lara empathized, she wasn't about to shrug off his inattentiveness. In her heart, she wanted a man who loved her more than his job.

"Life is never going to get less busy and relationships are like attending church, praying, and reading our Bibles. We have to make time for them. So, think about what you want to do and let me know." With that, she spun on her heel and continued her trek to the corral.

❧

Kevin watched Lara sashay out of the barn and decided women were a heap of trouble. She'd accused him of not caring, but he thought about Lara all the time. He'd even gone so far as to mention the idea of marrying her to Clayt. How'd she get it in her head that he didn't want a relationship with her?

He expelled a dismissive sigh. Fine. Let her be mad. Kevin wasn't going to let her wrap him around her little finger. He wasn't going to bend to her every whim. She'd walked in with an attitude today and decided to take it out on him. Great. Just great.

Irritation pumped through his veins and caused his temples to throb. He walked back to the office where he'd been working on a project. He'd told Ron at breakfast this morning that his gait was unsteady and each word coming out of his mouth felt as thick as maple syrup. Kevin had definitely been overdoing it, and he had to slow down. His neurologist gave him a list of warning signs to watch for, and if he noticed two or more, he had to readjust his schedule or suffer a setback. Fortunately, the Brambles understood. Ron offered him a desk job the next few days, and Kevin accepted.

Planting himself in the worn, leather chair, he stared at the spreadsheet before him. He had to admit that he felt rather wounded by Lara's terseness. He'd imagined an entirely different scenario. He thought she'd be happy to see him, and Kevin envisioned wrapping her in an embrace and kissing her pretty, pink lips.

Well, maybe she's just got up on the wrong side of the bed this morning.

He glanced at the bold-faced clock hanging on the wall. He'd give it until noon and see if she stopped in to apologize.

But noon came and went with no sign of Lara.

Making his way to the house for lunch, Kevin spotted her

and a few other volunteers sitting with the kids on the lawn. Colorful plastic thermal-lined lunch containers were strewn all around them. Kevin was tempted to grab his lunch and join them, but he sensed Lara wouldn't appreciate it. Even now, as he paused to stare in her direction, it seemed she deliberately ignored him. Kevin felt surprised at how much that hurt.

Deciding he wasn't hungry after all, he retreated to the office and sat there a little amazed at himself. If this was a taste of how his life would be without Lara, the outlook seemed bleak at best. He needed her. But when had that happened? He had never needed another human being before. When had Lara Donahue wheedled her way into his heart?

A tap sounded on the large glass window, interrupting Kevin's deliberations. He looked at the doorway to see the object of his thoughts standing not even ten feet away, holding a tray.

"Can I come in?"

"Sure."

She entered and set her burden on the corner of the desk. "Caroline wanted you to have some lunch, and since she's juggling several minor crises right now, I offered to bring it out here.

"Thanks."

"She made you a ham sandwich, sliced tomatoes, cucumbers, and a fat slice of peach pie."

With his insides so stirred up, it was hard to think about food.

Kevin rose to his feet. "Lara, please don't be angry with me. I'll try to do better, okay? A lot of this is new for me, the relationship thing. It shouldn't be at my age, I realize that. But it is."

She slipped her fingers into the front pockets of her blue jeans. "Okay."

Stepping around the desk, he pulled her hands back out and held them, one in each of his. Then he leaned forward and kissed her cheek. "I missed you, and believe it or not, you were never far from my thoughts."

"Well, Kevin, you have to tell me that. How else am I supposed to know? I can't read your mind." There was a sweetness in her voice that soothed his soul.

"I'll try to remember that."

"And you might want to look into a cell phone package that offers free nights and weekends." Lara cleared her throat.

"Point taken."

She gave him a grin.

"Now, can I have a hug? Man cannot live by Caroline Bramble's cooking alone."

&

Sunlight trickled through the flaming treetops as Kevin entered the church for Tim and Amanda's wedding. *They couldn't have asked for better weather*, Kevin decided as he claimed a seat in the second pew from the front. He had arrived early, and as they'd discussed last night at the rehearsal, Kevin's job was to save seats for some Donahue cousins who were driving in from Ohio today. Tim's parents and grandmother would sit in the pew in front of him, and Lara, a bridesmaid, would be standing in the front.

A small ensemble near the platform began to play their stringed instruments, and more guests filed into the sanctuary. Kevin willed his tense muscles to relax. He felt edgy, especially since last night's practice. While he knew it wasn't a big deal and it didn't mean anything, Kevin hadn't been able to stop a knot of envy from forming in his gut when he watched Lara walk up the aisle with her hand hooked around another man's elbow.

"Excuse me. This seat taken?"

Kevin turned to his left and grinned when he saw Brent. "What are you doing here?" He stood, and the two men shook hands.

"I told Polly I'd be her date for today." Brent scooted into the pew and sat beside Kevin. "Would you believe there's not another guy in all of Wisconsin who would escort her?"

"No, I wouldn't believe that."

"Me, neither. But here I am anyway."

Kevin chuckled. "Where's Polly?"

"Talking to some friends in the lobby." Brent unbuttoned the jacket of his black suit.

"Look at you, all dressed up. Spiffy lavender shirt. Where'd you find that?"

"Bought it."

"Did you buy the suit too, or is that rental?"

"I'll have you know I own my clothes, okay?"

Kevin laughed, and a few heads turned, so he quickly lowered his voice. "Well, if you never wear it again, they can always bury you in it."

"Yeah, that's what I figured too."

Kevin grinned. He'd forgotten how much fun it was to razz Brent. Phone calls just weren't the same.

"You're lookin' mighty spiffy yourself, Wink."

"Thanks." He tugged on the lapels of his jacket. "I'm meeting all of Lara's family today so I rented a tux."

"Cheapskate."

Kevin snickered at the quip.

"Polly tells me you and Lara are real serious."

"Yep. I'm going to marry her and live happily ever after."

"Asked her yet?"

"Not yet, but she knows it's coming. And she'll say 'yes.' I heard her talking to Polly about it awhile back."

"Well, I need to tell you something." Brent's voice sounded just above a whisper.

"About marrying Lara?" Kevin narrowed his gaze, studying his buddy's profile. Brent's jaw was clean shaven, and his dark brown hair appeared to have some special goop in it so it spiked up right above his forehead. Kevin wondered if the style of Brent's cut was that "bed-head" look that Lara said she disliked.

"I haven't been the friend you think."

"Shut up." Kevin stared straight ahead, knowing Lara would have told him if something had gone on between her and Brent.

"Wink, listen. . ."

Kevin whipped his gaze at him. "Do I have to remind you that you're in church?"

"I know where I am. In fact, I believe it's God who wants me to do this." He paused. "I need to apologize."

Kevin clenched his jaw.

"I purposely tried to make you jealous right from the start. I could see Lara cared for you that first day in your hospital room. I wished a girl would fawn all over me the way she fawned all over you. But back then, I was too proud and stubborn to admit it. So now I want to tell you I'm sorry."

"You serious?"

"Dead serious."

Kevin felt rather impressed. He could count the number of times on one hand that he'd heard Brent apologize. The recipients were all women, and Brent hadn't been genuinely repentant. In short, the act of contrition had served his purposes in one way or another.

But Kevin sensed this was very different.

"Apology accepted." He stuck out his right hand.

Brent clasped it, their gazes locked in silent challenge, then each man began to squeeze.

"Grip's still a little weak."

"Yeah, I'm workin' on it."

"Good. Wouldn't want you to turn into some kind of cream puff."

Kevin retracted his hand and grinned. "Not a chance."

People continued to fill the large, octagon-shaped sanctuary in anticipation of the ceremony. Polly showed up and claimed the seat beside Brent. Kevin found it amusing that the lilac print on her black dress matched Brent's attire.

Kevin leaned over to Brent. "Did you two do that on purpose?"

"Actually, no."

"Everyone's going to think you did."

"So what?"

Straightening in the pew, Kevin decided Brent must truly care for Polly if, number one, he agreed to miss a Saturday rodeoing to escort her to a wedding, and two, he didn't care that they looked like a set of bookends.

The Donahue cousins arrived, and after the usher brought them to the pew, Kevin introduced himself. Then, out of courtesy, he, Brent, and Polly slid down to the other end. Minutes later, a heavyset woman in a stylish skirt and blouse took a seat at the organ's keyboard, and the processional began. When Kevin caught sight of Lara in the flowing, emerald green dress, he had to force himself not to gape. Her light brown hair had been pinned up, but several tendrils spiraled down and brushed the tops of her shoulders. But along with admiration, Kevin felt a surge of jealousy rip through his being at the sight of the man guiding her down the aisle.

"Whoa, Boy. Easy now. That poor groomsman can't help it that he was picked to walk down the aisle with Lara. Your turn's coming."

Kevin's gaze slid to Brent. "When did you start mind-reading?"

"I didn't." Brent smirked. "But it wasn't hard to tell what you were thinking when you turned the color of Lara's gown."

Swallowing his laughter, Kevin realized how foolish he was behaving. He looked forward and found Lara's gaze on him. He sent her a wink. She smiled in return, and two pretty spots of pink appeared on her cheeks.

Brent leaned over again. "You've got nothing to worry about."

"You're right," he replied, feeling captivated as he regarded the woman with whom he planned to spend the rest of his life. "I don't."

twenty

Lara thought her younger brother's wedding day had been beautiful. The ceremony went off without a hitch, and the fall weather was perfect for outdoor pictures afterwards. Making the day all the more wonderful for Lara was the fact that her relatives and friends seemed to like Kevin. Then again, what wasn't to like? Handsome with an endearing limp that was becoming less noticeable with each passing week, Kevin charmed his way into the Donahue women's hearts and laughed and joked with the men as if he'd been part of the family forever. With Brent to egg him on, the cowboys were the life of the party—second only to the bride and groom.

By six o'clock, a scrumptious fare was served by candlelight in an elegant banquet room, and by eight, a shiny white limousine arrived to whisk the newlyweds to a undisclosed location. Tomorrow they planned to board a plane to Nova Scotia where they would honeymoon for the week.

"Tim and Amanda make such a sweet couple," Polly murmured.

Lara couldn't have agreed more as she stood outside the restaurant watching the limousine's taillights vanish into the night.

"But you know what I've learned?"

"What?" Lara looked at Polly.

"I've learned a bride-to-be can save a ton of money if she foregoes the DJ or live band."

"Are you still planning your wedding?"

"Sort of. I'm gathering data and deciding what I do and

don't like as far as ceremonies and receptions go. I even found my dress and put a down payment on it."

Lara chuckled. "You are so silly."

"I beg to differ." Polly raised her chin. "I'm trusting God to provide the groom. I don't know who he is, and I've given up trying to figure it out. I'm hanging onto Psalm thirty-seven, four."

Lara listened as Polly recited the passage.

"In other words, as I delight myself in the Lord, His desires become my desires." She smiled. "The Lord gave me that verse when I was feeling sorry for myself one night, Afterwards, I started thinking and soon concluded that Jesus has to be my First Love before I can have a husband."

"Sounds as if you're right on target." Lara gave her friend a smile.

"It's about time, eh?" Polly laughed. "Listen, it's freezing out here. Let's go in."

Lara agreed.

Reentering the building, Polly excused herself and headed for the ladies' restroom. Lara decided not to wait in the dim hallway and continued on to the banquet room where they'd left Kevin and Brent. But as she scanned the guests, she didn't see any sign of them. Spinning on her heel, she strolled back into the hallway. A heartbeat later, she thought she heard Kevin's voice and headed in that direction. She passed the restrooms until she came to another darkened corridor where she found Kevin and Brent deep in conversation. When they spotted her, however, neither man spoke another word.

"My apologies for interrupting."

She turned to walk away, but Kevin halted her.

"It's okay, Lara." He smiled and held out his right hand. Taking it, she stepped forward. "You should probably hear this too. Mac's up to her old tricks."

"Oh?" Lara glanced from Kevin to Brent.

"Mac says she's through talking. She's filing a lawsuit against Wink come Monday morning."

Lara frowned and looked back at Kevin. "But I thought Mr. Blivens said she didn't have a case."

In reply, Kevin expelled a weary-sounding sigh.

"She probably doesn't, but that woman's thinking is all backwards," Brent said. "She somehow believes that if she sues Wink, she'll get his attention. If she gets his attention, Mac thinks he'll marry her."

"Ain't gonna happen," Kevin drawled, giving Lara's hand a little squeeze. Gazing into her eyes, he added, "Guess I'll have to get a lawyer after all."

"Well, maybe not."

Lara and Kevin simultaneously glanced at Brent.

"Why don't you plan to attend the championship in Kentucky, Wink? They're looking for an announcer. We all think you'd fit that part, and if you accepted the position, you could still rodeo."

Lara ignored the cry of opposition from her heart. She sensed Kevin cared for her in a special way, but she felt certain she couldn't compete with the rodeo.

"What's attending the finals got to do with Mac?" Kevin asked, letting go of Lara's hand and causing her to wonder if the gesture was indicative of his true feelings.

Brent grinned. "I've got a plan." He caught sight of Polly who appeared in the corridor's entryway, then looked back at Kevin. "I'll tell you 'bout it later."

Disappointment filled Lara's being. She would like to have heard Brent's "plan."

The four of them ambled back to the reception area and socialized for a bit longer. Lara tried to enjoy herself but all the while, as she stood at Kevin's side, she feared losing him to what he loved most. . .the life of a pro rodeo cowboy.

❧

Fall continued on its course with sunshine, dry air, and cool temperatures. The days and weeks went by in a whir as Lara continued her job at the hospital, but she spent most of her free time at the ranch. She helped Kevin with chores, although it was obvious he didn't need her anymore. A social worker who loved people, Lara realized her deepest desire was to be needed. However, with Kevin on the mend, surpassing even the doctors' prognoses, he could pull his own weight at The Regeneration Ranch.

She attempted to convey those very thoughts to Kevin one evening.

"Lara, you know what your problem is? You think too much." He tossed her a smirk before disappearing behind one of the two horses the Brambles had recently purchased.

"I'm just trying to tell you how I feel." Exasperated, Lara scooped up a handful of straw and threw it at him.

Moments later, Kevin emerged around the backside of the mare, his blond hair and the shoulders of his red plaid shirt littered with prickly shafts. Lara had to swallow a laugh.

"I already know how you feel."

She raised her chin.

"But now you're gonna get it."

Seeing the glint of determination in his blue eyes, she bolted out of the barn. It dawned on her then that the one thing Kevin couldn't manage yet was to outrun her.

❧

Since October was "Brain Injury Awareness" month at County General, special on-going seminars were held for the general public, and Kevin's doctors asked him to speak at one of them. Lara felt so proud of Kevin's progress, and she thanked God every day for answering her prayers and healing him.

Yet, despite those many uplifting and fun times they shared, discouragement began to nibble away at Lara's sense of peace. Kevin skirted discussions about the future, which only inflated her insecurities about the two of them. He now said he loved her, and Lara could see in eyes that he meant each word. But she wondered if Kevin struggled with the idea of commitment. Determined to find the answer, she applied both their personality traits and their situation to every psychological evaluation she'd learned in school, although she only felt more confused at their inconclusiveness. At last, she decided Kevin was right. She *did* think too much. From that point on, she once again endeavored to give her fears to God and leave them in His all-powerful grip.

Polly, on the other hand, proved to be very little support, since she was distracted beyond reason by a certain handsome bull rider. She soon spouted off PRCA standings with the proficiency of a doctor rattling off lab orders. However, because of her influence, Brent had "settled down," to the amazement of his friends. Best of all, he asked Jesus into his heart, and no one could have been happier to hear the news than Kevin—with Polly running a close second.

At long last, November arrived, and Kevin couldn't stop talking about the finals in Kentucky. In fact, Lara likened his excitement to a little boy at Christmastime. But, as ironic as it seemed, his happiness only saddened her all the more. To her, it appeared that his former lifestyle still possessed his heart, and Lara wondered if it would ever belong to her.

"Lara, I'm not fool enough to entertain thoughts of bareback riding again." Kevin leaned his back up against the side of her car and folded his arms. Rays from a faraway autumn sun shone through the now-barren treetops near the Brambles' gravel driveway. "What are you worried about?"

"I'm not worried." It was the biggest fib she'd ever told, and

Kevin's expression said he saw right through it. Lowering her gaze, Lara kicked at the stones beneath her brown, high-heeled pumps. She was still dressed in her Sunday attire, having come right to the ranch after church this morning so she and Kevin could have some time together.

"I don't need or want a mother hen clucking at me the rest of my life."

Is that how he sees me? A mother hen? Clucking?

Lara felt the blood drain from her head and stop somewhere in her chest. Her heart threatened to explode with anguish.

"I apologize, Kev. I never meant to *cluck*."

He had the audacity to laugh.

"You know, if it bothered you so much, you could have said something sooner." Lara felt like she was choking on each word. "When people talk to each other it's called *communication*."

A little frown knitted his brows. "Are you angry?"

"Why would I be angry?" The reply dripped with sarcasm. "You only called me a clucking mother hen and said you didn't want to spend the rest of your life with me."

Kevin pushed himself off the car. "I said no such thing."

Lara stomped around to the driver's side, but before she could fish her keys from her purse, Kevin caught her arm and spun her around to face him. By that time, however, she felt so wounded, tears leaked from her eyes.

"What's wrong?" He cupped her face and brought her gaze to his. "Are you crying?"

"You're a genius." She sniffed back an ounce of emotion.

Kevin swiveled around so her back was to the Brambles' farmhouse. "Cut it out, Lara. If Ron sees that I made you cry, he'll come out here with his shotgun."

She laughed in spite of herself. Ron was such a peaceable man that she wasn't sure he even owned a shotgun.

"There. That's better. You're pretty when you smile. I mean, you're pretty when you cry too. It's just that I like it better when you're happy."

His stammering caused her to grin.

"Now, look, I didn't mean to hurt your feelings. But I've told you before I'm not going to ride again."

"I know. That's not what I'm worried about." Lara wiped the moisture off her cheeks with her fingertips. "I've been trying to tell you for weeks that I feel like the rodeo is the love of your life."

"Not so. Jesus has the number one slot."

"I'm talking about second to our Savior. It's the rodeo, not me. At the finals, I'm afraid you'll get around the rest of the cowboys, remember the thrill of that eight-second ride, and you won't want to come back home."

"Home." A rueful smile curved his mouth. "This city, you. . .I'm really home, aren't I? Maybe I shouldn't have ever left."

His soft words tenderized her heart.

"Look, Lara, you've got nothing to fear. I'm not going to ride again. Ever."

"What if your friends find something else for you to do?"

Kevin shook his head. "I never thought I'd say it, but you're acting like an irrational female. All this time I thought you were levelheaded."

"That just proves you don't know me very well." Hurt mingled with irritation and coursed through her veins. Glancing at the leather purse slung over her shoulder, she shoved her hand inside it and rummaged for her car keys.

Kevin grasped her upper arms and brought her around to stand in front of him. "I know you as well as I know anybody. Look at me."

Lara slowly raised her gaze to meet his unwavering stare.

"I love you. And this weekend at the finals, you'll see that I love you more than any rodeo. Even more than a championship."

"I don't want to go anymore." The truth was she hadn't wanted to go in the first place.

"Hey!" He gave her a gentle shake. "Do you love me?"

"Yes."

"Okay, then." He grinned. "You just keep practicing. That's the right answer."

Lara wrenched herself free of his hold and gave him a playful sock in the arm.

❧

"There you are!" Polly came running at Lara at a full gallop. "Where have you been?"

Lara turned and pointed toward the refreshment stand. "I was in—"

"Come on!" Polly grabbed her wrist and led her into Freedom Hall, the midsection part of the vast Exposition Center. "Oh, Sister, if you missed this, Kevin would never speak to me again."

"You?" Lara was hard-pressed to keep up with her friend.

"Yeah, it's my job to make sure you're standing in this particular aisle at this particular time." Polly glanced at her watch. "Whew! I think we might even be three minutes early."

Lara didn't even ask. By now, she knew something was up—and she knew that "something" involved Mackenzie Sabino. For the past two days, the woman had all but planted herself in Kevin's path so he practically tripped over her. But that neither surprised nor upset Lara. She actually felt sorry for Mac. The petite blond fell into that "poor little rich girl" typecast, and she thought she could buy anything she wanted, including Kevin's love. Moreover, Mac was obviously used to getting her own way and would rather wield manipulative threats than take no for an answer.

"Ladies and gentlemen, may I please have your undivided attention?"

Lara grinned at the announcer's Kentucky drawl.

"Back in June, our own Kevin Wincouser, known as 'Wink' to most all of us, got bucked off a horse and took a bad spill during a competition. He suffered what's called a traumatic brain injury."

"Yeah, and good thing he landed on his head, or he might have really hurt himself."

Glancing over her shoulder, she saw Brent walk up the aisle and stand next to Polly. Lara rolled her eyes at his smart remark, but several folks in the stands heard it and laughed.

"As a result of his accident," the announcer continued, "I'm sad to say Wink's rodeo days are gone forever."

The crowd moaned and booed.

"But he's here tonight to say goodbye to his fans and friends alike. . .and here he comes right now."

To her left, Lara watched as a lone figure of a man walked into the ring, leading a dapple gray horse behind him.

"Where's Mac?" Brent wanted to know.

"Sitting in the most expensive seat in the house, of course." Polly laughed.

Lara arched a brow. "This is all for Mac's benefit, I take it?"

"No. No, it isn't," Brent said. His somber expression told Lara he spoke the truth. "But this public farewell will put an end to Mac's plans right quick. Trust me."

"Okay." Lara was all for any solution that halted Mac Sabino's scheming ways.

Kevin came to stand in the center of the ring. The big-screen "Jumbotron" magnified his entrance for all to see. He stopped and waved to the now-cheering crowd, then, once the noise level dropped, he began to speak into the microphone he evidently wore on the collar of his chambray shirt.

"I want to thank you all for your support over the years and for your prayers over the last five months. I mean it when I say it's by God's grace that I'm standing here, talking to you. But I had top-notch physicians, the best of friends, and I even found a brand new family who helped me get through some tough times. Now I'm ready to start a new life. But there's just one thing I have to do first, so you'll have to pardon this rather personal moment."

Kevin cleared his throat and turned Lara's way, pinning her with his blue-eyed gaze.

"Lara Beth Donahue, I love you, and I'm asking you to be my wife. Will you marry me?"

Freedom Hall grew suddenly so quiet, everyone in attendance could hear a coin that clattered on the cement floor. But Lara couldn't get herself to move, let alone utter a syllable. She felt paralyzed by a strange mixture of awe and embarrassment.

Kevin took a step forward, his expression one of earnestness. "Lara, I need you."

Those were the very words she longed to hear.

Just then, Brent leaned over. "Honey, the world is watching. If you say no, Wink's in big trouble."

Lara shook off her shock. "I'm not going to turn him down. Are you crazy? I've been waiting half my life for this!"

Stepping past the grinning security personnel, Lara ran out to Kevin and flung herself into his outstretched arms. The cheers and whistles from the crowd were deafening, but Lara managed to hear Kevin's chuckles.

"So are you going to marry me or not?" His lips brushed her ear.

"Yes, I'll marry you," Lara replied with tears of joy in her eyes. "A thousand times yes!"

Wearing a triumphant smile, Kevin mounted the horse and pulled Lara up into the saddle behind him. Together they circled the arena, and Kevin waved to the bystanders. Lara thought it was as perfect an ending to his rodeo career as riding off into the sunset was to a good Western. But in reality, they had found love. They had found each other.

Even though Kevin had taken the long ride home.

A Letter To Our Readers

Dear Reader:

In order that we might better contribute to your reading enjoyment, we would appreciate your taking a few minutes to respond to the following questions. We welcome your comments and read each form and letter we receive. When completed, please return to the following:

Fiction Editor
Heartsong Presents
PO Box 719
Uhrichsville, Ohio 44683

1. Did you enjoy reading *The Long Ride Home* by Andrea Boeshaar?
   ❑ Very much! I would like to see more books by this author!
   ❑ Moderately. I would have enjoyed it more if

   _____

   _____

   _____

2. Are you a member of **Heartsong Presents**? ❑ Yes ❑ No
   If no, where did you purchase this book? _____

   _____

3. How would you rate, on a scale from 1 (poor) to 5 (superior), the cover design? _____

4. On a scale from 1 (poor) to 10 (superior), please rate the following elements.

   ____ Heroine   ____ Plot
   ____ Hero   ____ Inspirational theme
   ____ Setting   ____ Secondary characters

5. These characters were special because?_____
_____
_____

6. How has this book inspired your life?_____
_____
_____

7. What settings would you like to see covered in future
   Heartsong Presents books? _____
_____
_____

8. What are some inspirational themes you would like to see
   treated in future books? _____
_____
_____

9. Would you be interested in reading other **Heartsong
   Presents** titles? ❑ Yes ❑ No

10. Please check your age range:
   ❑ Under 18   ❑ 18-24
   ❑ 25-34   ❑ 35-45
   ❑ 46-55   ❑ Over 55

Name _____
Occupation _____
Address _____
City_____ State_____ Zip_____

Kaleidoscope

4 stories in 1

*P*erspective changes in four suspense-filled romances by Lauralee Bliss, Gloria Brandt, DiAnn Mills, and Kathleen Paul.

Contemporary novels of mystery, suspense, love, and faith follow the lives of four women who wonder just how much of their hearts they can share with their romantic interests.

Contemporary, paperback, 480 pages, 5 ³/₁₆" x 8"

❤ ❤ ❤ ❤ ❤ ❤ ❤ ❤ ❤ ❤ ❤ ❤ ❤ ❤

❤ ❤ ❤ ❤ ❤ ❤ ❤ ❤ ❤ ❤ ❤ ❤ ❤ ❤

Presents

Great Inspirational Romance at a Great Price!

Heartsong Presents books are inspirational romances in contemporary and historical settings, designed to give you an enjoyable, spirit-lifting reading experience. You can choose wonderfully written titles from some of today's best authors like Hannah Alexander, Andrea Boeshaar, Yvonne Lehman, Tracie Peterson, and many others.

When ordering quantities less than twelve, above titles are $3.25 each.
Not all titles may be available at time of order.

JEARTSONG ♥ PRESENTS
Love Stories
Are Rated G!

That's for godly, gratifying, and of course, great! If you love a thrilling love story but don't appreciate the sordidness of some popular paperback romances, **Heartsong Presents** is for you. In fact, **Heartsong Presents** is the premiere inspirational romance book club featuring love stories where Christian faith is the primary ingredient in a marriage relationship.

Sign up today to receive your first set of four, never-before-published Christian romances. Send no money now; you will receive a bill with the first shipment. You may cancel at any time without obligation, and if you aren't completely satisfied with any selection, you may return the books for an immediate refund!

Imagine. . .four new romances every four weeks—two historical, two contemporary—with men and women like you who long to meet the one God has chosen as the love of their lives. . .all for the low price of $10.99 postpaid.

To join, simply complete the coupon below and mail to the address provided. **Heartsong Presents** romances are rated G for another reason: They'll arrive Godspeed!

YES! Sign me up for Hearts♥ng!

NEW MEMBERSHIPS WILL BE SHIPPED IMMEDIATELY!
Send no money now. We'll bill you only $10.99 postpaid with your first shipment of four books. Or for faster action, call toll free 1-800-847-8270.

NAME_____

ADDRESS_____

CITY_____ STATE_____ ZIP_____

MAIL TO: HEARTSONG PRESENTS, P.O. Box 721, Uhrichsville, Ohio 44683
or visit www.heartsongpresents.com